Alice in Corporateland

Also by Joan Wendland

Let's Fall in Love 'til Wednesday

Praise for *Alice in Corporateland*

Alice traded a Cinderella glass slipper for tough corporate shoe leather and got a prince of a satire.

Administrative Assistant to His Highness of Corporateland
Name withheld for obvious reasons

––––––––––

Breaking news for anyone out of work, unemployed or outsourced: your job has been transferred to a contemporary version of Wonderland in author Joan Wendland's book. Drop down the rabbit hole into a paper pit to re-apply—in fact, the duchess has authorized payment to you of two cents an hour to be a tenth-level paper pusher.

If you want to rise on the corporate ladder, be prepared to contend with all those critters over your head keeping you down, including the lecherous lizard and the Dodo, who is your job-trainer-in-chief, who will twist you in knots. If you can't wake up soon (and you can't!), you'll never get back home in time for your next job interview, especially with the Duchess of Downsteepysizing demanding "Off with her head."

In these pages you'll find the job of your dreams, or rather, the corporate job of your worst nightmares. This is biting, funny, and satirical.

Paul Davids
Executive Producer of Showtime's *Roswell* and Producer/Director of Universal's *The Sci-Fi Boys*

––––––––––

I'm reminded of my time in my own Corporateland. This provides entertaining comic relief but makes edgy points on the absurdity of seemingly intelligent business practices. Satire with a bite on job layoffs and unemployment.

Bonnie Norris, HR Specialist with a Fortune 500 Company
Company name withheld by request

––––––––––

Joan Wendland's book entitled "Alice in Corporateland" is a well written and well researched (no doubt with the years that she spent in the corporate world) satire of the sometimes difficult to understand and incomprehensible modes in which business is managed and conducted in modern America. There are elements in which I can personally relate and, thank goodness, situations and types of people that I have learned to avoid over the course of my experience in white collar America. The picture that is painted is surely one that anyone who has worked in an office will enjoy.

Christopher G. Cook
Director, Strategic Accounts
Company name withheld

Joan's treatment of the corporate workplace is humorous with a nice satirical touch and brings to mind what was said of Jonathan Swift when he peeled back the pomposity and self importance of his peers in seventeenth-century England: he provided the reader with the "shock of recognition."

Joan's storytelling is poignant and reminds me of the many personality types that I've encountered during my time in the working world for the last thirty-five years. Although many corporate environments give more than lip service to the dignity of the employee, some do not. Joan's manuscript reveals the frustrations and hypocrisy of the workplace dominated, unfortunately, by some really bizarre people. Alice wonders if the Grand Dodo Bird who is the training officer "has a self image problem because he's at an evolutionary dead end."

Alice learns quickly after her fall into the pit that meritorious performance is not rewarded and thinking for one's self is risky. But this manuscript is not about defeatism. The craziness she encounters convinces her to get out. As Lenny the Lizard advised "best get doing done if she was ever to get out of here." Being cut loose from the herd is a scary proposition but after confronting weirdness in something as important as employment, the reader is relieved that Alice is not subdued but is determined to succeed. In Alice's case, the corporate vision statement is suitable for framing and not much else.

Alice in Corporate Land is a delightfully thoughtful read and would be a provocative addition to any corporate training curriculum.

Bob Hendricks
Former Positions:
City Manager, Sheridan, Oregon
Human Resources Director, McMinnville, Oregon
Medical Clinic Administrator, Astoria, Oregon
Content Director, PersonPlanet.Com, Wilsonville, Oregon

Alice in Corporateland

A Curiouser and Curiouser Bizness

Joan Wendland

iUniverse, Inc.
Bloomington

Alice in Corporateland
A Curiouser and Curiouser Bizness

iUniverse books may be ordered through booksellers or by contacting:

iUniverse
1663 Liberty Drive
Bloomington, IN 47403
www.iuniverse.com
1-800-Authors (1-800-288-4677)

ISBN: 978-1-4502-7334-3 (sc)
ISBN: 978-1-4502-7335-0 (dj)
ISBN: 978-1-4502-7336-7 (ebk)

Library of Congress Control Number: 2010917399

Printed in the United States of America

iUniverse rev. date: 12/23/2010

To anyone ever rightsized, downsized, or reengineered out of a job, and to those left clutching their computer chips.

With apologies to Lewis Carroll.
And to the animals for assigning them human behaviors.

Note: No animals were harmed during the writing of this story. All agreed to be trained for this tale.

"If you don't know where you are going,
  you might wind up some place else."

—Yogi Berra

Into the Paper Pit

The living-room clock chimed. Alice was late. No doubt about it. She was late. Instead of rushing out the door, she settled more deeply into the cushions on the couch. She gnashed her teeth against the job interview that loomed, her first in twenty years. *Just fifteen more minutes*, she thought, *and if I hurry I'll still be on time.*

She absorbed the comfort of the cushions cupped around her. Into the reflection in the mirror over the fireplace, she mouthed, *Well, Alice, where are you going?* Her reflection had no answers, only the same questions.

Who? What? Where? The reign of Prince Executive Charming was over. Alice's glass slipper lay on the floor of her closet smashed into teeny tiny pieces, and there is nothing quite so broken as glass. Broken too was her belief that marriage and the prince were her everlasting happy dance.

She knew how to be a corporate wife, but all those ways were the prince's ways. Now which way? She crossed all of her fingers over the impending interview.

She sighed again and closed her eyes. *Just for a tiny minute*, she thought. Her head nodded and her chin hit her chest with a thump. The clock chimed again. Alice's eyes flipped open to the hands on the clock. Fifteen minutes had become thirty! "Oh dear, I'm really late," she said.

"You are late. You are terribly late," a voice said. Alice turned quickly. Peering through her patio window was a white rabbit—a large white rabbit with tall ears dressed in a pin-striped suit. Alice rubbed the sleep out of her eyes and looked again. The rabbit stood there staring at her with glassy red eyes. He tapped an enormous gold watch dangling from a chain.

Alice tapped on the window. "Shoo. Go away." Alice was used to cute little brown bunnies hopping across her yard, but not white rabbits dressed in a business suit like the prince wore. *I must be hallucinating*, she thought.

"You are late. You are terribly late," he said and hopped away upright on polished black wing tips past the fine wood planters with their trailing vines.

She shook her head to clear the vision. *I'm just overly anxious over the job interview*, she thought, *and now I'm really really late.* She jammed on her high-heeled boots, grabbed her car keys, and ran to the garage. The garage was empty! She must have left the car in the drive. The door rolled up on an empty drive and the staring white rabbit. "Follow me," he said.

"That's absurd. You're not even real. You're just a figment of my hallucination."

"Are you sure?" he said, holding out a paw. "Touch me and see."

Alice tentatively put a hand out and pulled it back, then straightened her shoulders. She'd show this hallucination a thing or two. She rubbed her hands together and prepared to brush away the vision of the rabbit. Instead of thin air she connected with a furry paw and a solid body.

She jumped back two feet and yelled, "You're real!"

The rabbit retorted smugly, "Told ya."

Alice gulped, put both hands on her hips, and jabbed her index finger at his furry face. "And just why would I follow a talking rabbit, huh? You just tell me that."

"Because you are late for your interview, and I know a shortcut."

"How do you know about my interview?"

"I work for the company where you are interviewing." He put four feet to the ground, front furry paws followed by two leather wing tips. Thumpty thud. Thumpty thud. He carefully avoided the damp, evenly clipped grass edging the double drive. Not a spot of dampness besmirched his shiny shoes or his flapping pinstripes. He paused and looked back at Alice. "Follow me. I'll get you there on time."

Alice's head swiveled between the white rabbit at the end of the drive and the top of the drive where the car should have been. She wondered, *Is this just an absurd dream where anything can happen that doesn't make sense, and then I wake up when it gets to the end? Or did I wander off the pages of one fairy tale into another?*

It *was* absurd following a talking rabbit. *I know I am late,* she reasoned, *but if I run very very hard, I am sure to catch up.* She further reasoned that he was nicely dressed for a rabbit, and she thought the watch was an unusual antique gold piece. She was always making excuses to make it seem she'd done the right thing. She hitched up her skirt and ran.

A white signpost popped up at the end of Happily Ever After Lane. This Way it read and pointed in the direction of the rabbit. She let out the breath she had been holding. This at least was some confirmation she was going the right way. She smiled ruefully at the name of the lane. Nothing is forever. It should have been an omen when she had moved here with the prince twenty years ago. She brushed that thought away and ran.

She ran as fast as her legs, unused to running after rabbits, could run. The hem of her blue skirt flapped around her boot tops. The blue paisley scarf atop her periwinkle sweater streamed behind her. She ran along the trimmed hedgerow to the end of Happily Ever After Lane.

Another white signpost popped out of the ground at the crossroad. Every inch of the post was filled with arrows pointing up to the sky, down into the ground, right, left, in circles, and in between. Alice twisted her head every which way in order to read them, hoping for a clue. "This Way. That Way. This and That Way. One Way or Another. Right Way. Wrong Way. Every Which Way. Everyone Else's Way. Not Your Way. This Way In, No Way Out. All the Ways Are Ours, Not Yours. Go Around in Circles."

Her brain was as jumbled as the arrows. *Now which way?* She sighed with relief when she caught the glint of the rabbit's watch on the block ahead. In a split-second decision, she followed the glint. Her feet slapped the asphalt and her mind jumped as she ran after the rabbit.

The glint made niggling little doubts pop on and off in her brain. The prince had had glint and flash and sparkle too. He ran too. Straight up the corporate ladder. See Alice watch him run. See Alice gaze adoringly as he runs. See Alice cook. See Alice clean. See Alice iron the prince's shirts. See Alice iron her mind flat.

At least the rabbit was going somewhere—hopefully to her job interview, if what he said was true.

Alice puffed. She panted. She wished she had changed to her jogging shoes. She was used to jogging three miles a day, but not in high heels after fast rabbits. But on she ran: over the bridge, past the creek, through the subdivision, past Happy Valley village limits. Thunder rumbled behind her. Alice looked back. Dark, threatening clouds were moving over Happy Valley in the direction they were running. Her breath swelled to a large pain in her chest. Sweat ran in rivulets down her face.

Raindrops pinged against her skin. Her sides and throat ached. Her legs felt like she'd been pedaling a bike uphill for hours.

Just then the rabbit stopped in front of a sign. Crematorium Row. Alice shuddered. A second later he hopped to a garbage can on the other side of the road, lifted the lid, and appeared to disappear underneath.

Once she stood closer to the sign, she noticed that it read Corporatoreum Row. Alice expelled a held breath. She'd misread the sign. Corporatoreum didn't sound bad at all, and the letters were soothing and green. It was not what she thought! Water foamed over piled boulders into a pond. A clump of willow trees swayed gracefully over the rain-dotted water. Gold and white chrysanthemums nestled among the rocks. Bermed grassy lawns rolled beyond the sign. *This couldn't be that bad, could it?*

The sky got darker. The thunder rumbled louder. The raindrops grew bigger and closer together. Alice slid the garbage can aside. A dark hole disappeared into the bowels of the Earth. Maybe it was some kind of underground shelter. One thing was certain: if she stayed out here, she would be drenched. Alice hiked up her skirt and plunged into the darkness.

As her eyes adjusted to the dark, she saw a sloping, dimly lit path into the earth. At first she wondered where she was going, but then she saw the flash of the rabbit's watch. She followed him.

She tripped on a tree root and tumbled headfirst, bumping the sides, which dipped and then plummeted straight down. Wind chopped at her face and mouth. She was so scared, her breath jammed in her throat and cut off the scream there. Her arms and legs splayed against the up-draft. She looked down. It made her dizzy; she couldn't see the bottom. *I think I am falling so far I must be on my way to the center of the Earth.* Something caught her eye as she continued to plummet. She looked around. Everywhere she swiveled her head she saw paper. Rows and stacks and sheets of paper. Pieces bound, bundled, spindled, and collated. Stapled, crumpled, double-sided, and single-sheeted. Letters and memos, printouts and reports with numbers so numerous and tiny they filled all the white spaces. Stacks were

Xeroxed and senselessly repeated. There were Post-Its and messages and shredded strips with words deleted. File drawers rolled out at her like nasty tongues filled with more separated sheets. Three-hole-punched paper snowed dots on her.

Down, down she fell. Just when she wondered if this would ever end, she slammed into the ground. She bounced once and then got her footing. No sooner did she catch her balance than she stepped on a stack of loose papers. The paper slid underfoot and sent her sprawling. She lay on the ground a bit dazed. She wiggled finger, arm, and leg joints. Surprisingly she didn't hurt, though it seemed she should, having just fallen to the center of the Earth. She looked around. Piles and boxes of paper were stacked everywhere. *Center of the Earth? Center of a Staples stockroom was more like it.*

The rabbit appeared in front of her twitching his whiskers while tapping his watch. "You're late. You're late," he said. He had tall ears, taller than her head, though his head was shorter than her shoulders. His nose sat off-center on his face as if a punch had rearranged its original placement. Instead of being cute, pink, and pert like most rabbits' noses, it was a lumpy stub like a large wart. Her eyes crossed looking at it.

"You're late. You're late," he repeated. He tapped his watch. Alice took a step back and uncrossed her eyes. She peered at his watch. "Why, it has no hands. How can I be late when it can't tell time?"

"Precisely my point. You've run out of time. You are too old. No experience. Not enough education. But you are a sturdy girl. You can process paper."

"Too old?" Alice replied. "I'm forty-something, never mind what, and well past the girl stage, I might add."

The rabbit nodded as if she'd just proven his point. "Just as I said. Too old, and no experience."

No experience? She'd done a lot in those forty years. "What about life experience?"

"That is of no consequence. It doesn't count," he said.

Her shoulders slumped. That is just what the prince had told her. After years of living in the prince's shadow, she found that only he was important, but she was not. She could see that arguing with the rabbit was getting her nowhere, just as it had with the prince. "What is paper processing, and why would I want to do it?"

"Because this is Corporateland, and as anyone with a grain of intelligence knows, Corporateland is built on paper. You are privileged to be here to work at its very foundation. You are not equipped for any of the higher positions, but it just so happens by the most fortunate of circumstances that we have a position open in the paper pit for generic paper clerk number ten." The rabbit looked her up and down. "Any addle-brain can do it."

Alice frowned. The rabbit didn't seem to notice. He kept right on talking. "Room for advancement. Only nine levels up and you'll be generic paper clerk number one. And you have arrived at just the right time because, as you know, you are late. You are—"

"Yes, yes," Alice interrupted. "You told me that." She paused. If she made him cross, the rabbit might leave, and then she'd never find her way out. Best to be polite. She tipped her head and lowered her eyes, even though she didn't feel polite. "If you don't mind, I would just like to leave, so if you could just show me the way out, I won't bother you any more. I need to get to my interview."

"Interview? You just had it. And the only way out of here is through the paper," the rabbit informed her as he rubbed his furry front paws together. His red eyes gleamed.

Alice gritted her teeth and spit out, "Interview? Interview? *That* was an interview? You tricked me."

With a self-satisfied smirk, he said, "You followed. It was your own decision."

A deep roar threatened to erupt from her throat, but she clamped it back. She clenched her fists and decided on her most reasonable, logical approach. Surely a voice of reason resided in his rabbit head. The rabbit was right in a way, she *had* followed him, which she regretted now. She *was* used to following others. First King Daddy, then Prince Executive.

"Oh my goodness," Alice said, though she was at a loss to figure out what good there was in any of this. She'd make the best of it until she figured a way out. Then again, it was not every day one met a talking rabbit, and he had cleared up in a way what she was late for, and she did get out of the rain. Here she was again, justifying what she'd done to make it seem right. But now that she was here, she'd do what he wanted so she could leave. "What is it that you want me to do for you?"

"Why, organize all this paper, of course. Use your head. A pretty little head it is too," he said. He tilted one of his ears very close to one of hers and reached a paw around her shoulders and gave them a none-too-comforting squeeze.

Alice's stomach lurched. *He's a prime candidate for* The Ick Factor *reality show*, she thought. "You shouldn't touch me personally like that, it's very impolite."

"You misunderstand my intentions," he said as he combed one side of his whiskers with the index and middle fingers of one paw. "I have a PhD in management."

She ducked her head and tried to hide her flushed cheeks. *After all, he* is *an animal, and I am human*, she reasoned. "What is it you want me to do?"

"Do is for you to do. Do I have to tell you everything?"

"But ... but ... I don't remember you telling me anything at all," she spluttered.

"I've told you something, and that is not nothing," the rabbit said and pulled his chest up till tufts of fur popped out of the shirt on his chest.

Alice sighed, but she was also being practical, so she said, "Well, I am sure I can figure something out if you will tell me a few things. I need to know what your system is now. How do you use the paper? Is some stored in different sections? Who uses it? Things like that."

He blinked his red eyes and rolled them to the top of his head. "You listen to nothing I tell you. I just want you to create a system to organize it. Not necessary, not necessary at all for you to know those other things."

Alice thought quickly. "If I organize this, then can I leave? Then will you show me the way out?"

He seemed to be listening, but his red eyes bounced from one corner of the corridor to the other and then to someplace over Alice's head. "Yes. Yes. Whatever," he replied and hopped away.

Feeling less than confident about his distracted

agreement, Alice looked all around her and tried to decide where to begin. It did seem a backward way of working though, not knowing all the pieces before she tried to put them together.

The narrow tunnel that she'd just fallen through opened into a cavernous room. A pit really. A paper pit. Her heart sank and then hit her shoes. She could never, ever organize this in her entire lifetime. Huge stone pillars grew out of the concrete floor and traveled to the ceiling three floors up. Above, below, and all around her was paper, just like the tunnel except that the boxes, stacks, bundles, and pallets were on row after row of shelves stacked to the ceiling in either direction.

She groaned. *Matches*, she thought. *I need boxes and boxes of matches.* She giggled hysterically. She'd give the rabbit a huge organized pile of ashes. She straightened her lips, wrapped both arms around her middle, and groaned again. How was she ever going to get out of here?

Weak spotlights shown down from the ceiling. Specks of paper dust floated in the pale shafts. The dim light threw dark shadows into every corner. Gray walls surrounded her. She traced an index finger along a shelf in front of her. It was coated with gray dust. She walked between the shelves and ran straight into an enormous dusty spider's web draped from one side to the other. She shuddered and brushed it from her face.

The Bleeping Rabbit and the Bleeping Lizard

Bleep. Bleep. Bleep. The sound echoed from the far wall. It was that same annoying bleep that garbage trucks use when backing from alleys. The bleeping came closer. She stuck fingers in each ear. At the end of the row, a gray lizard drove a forklift with two large prongs sticking from it. He pressed buttons on a key pad, and the prongs shoved under a pallet of papers on a shelf and extracted them. He reversed the operation and moved the pallet to another shelf. He did this six different times, moving the same pallet to six different spots. She walked over to the truck and unplugged her ears, "Could you stop that bleeping noise for just a minute?"

His head was bald. Tough scales covered his skin. Though lizards are usually slim and trim, this one had a large belly that spilled through the openings in the steering wheel. His tongue incessantly flicked in and out of his head. "You must be the new skirt the rabbit hired," he said.

"Alice. My name is Alice," she said. "And you are?"

"Lenny, just call me Lenny."

"Could you just tell me why you are moving the same pallet of papers back and forth?"

"Sure, Skirt, to—"

Alice interrupted. "My name is not Skirt. How would you like it if I addressed you 'Hey, Pants?'"

"Hey, I was just kidding, Skirt." He stretched his lips thin and tight in some facsimile of a smile. "Gotta have a sense of humor if you work around here. Me and U Nick got good senses of humor. You gotta learn to take a joke."

"Eunuch? Who's the eunuch?" asked Alice.

"The rabbit. U Nick the rabbit. Don't you know anything, Skirt?"

"Well, there was so much running and talking we didn't exchange names."

"Just to show you there's no hard feelings, I'll give you a little tip. Don't ever call the rabbit U Nick to his face. We all do behind his back. Story is he got the name from a stint in the army. That first day, his sergeant went down the line inspecting the troops. Each was supposed to bark back a name when the sergeant stopped in front of him. Seems Nick wasn't attentive enough. The sergeant stopped, thunked an index finger at Nick's chest, and yelled, 'You!'"

"'Nick,' he said, forgetting the sir and snapping to. Every time after that, they'd go through the same routine rapid-fire style till the sergeant's 'you' and Nick's 'Nick' were a name. U Nick. He had to take it then. But I advise you, don't use it to his face now. He may be short, but those back legs carry a powerful kick. You catch my drift, Skirt?" He ran his eyes up and down her frame. His tongue flicked in and out.

A shiver ran across her shoulders and raised prickly bumps on her arms. "Lenny, could you please keep your tongue in your mouth when talking to me?"

"Are you discriminating against my species?"

"Oh, no," Alice said, "It's just that I find it disrespectful. It's rude and demeaning, and I would like you to stop doing it."

"You have a thing or two to learn. This is a characteristic of lizards," he said, his tongue flicking even faster. "If you continue with this discrimination, I'll have to report you."

Since her goal was to get out of here, she said nothing more but muttered under her breath, "Surely there are other lizards around to flick his tongue at."

She turned away and then back again. "Could you just tell me one thing? Why are you moving the same pallet over and over again?"

"So U Nick sees that I get doing done," he said, sitting up straighter on the forklift. "I am the master paper pusher. You've got a lot to learn, Skirt. You best get your own doing done. U Nick likes an organized pit." He made a U-turn midaisle and bleeped off in a puff of gray dust.

Turning around, she noticed a desk neatly arrayed with pens and pencils and a computer and phone outside what she assumed was the rabbit's office. Her desk, she supposed, and she felt a flash of gratitude that one was prepared for her arrival. She tested the chair and ducked her head to check the contents of the drawers. A voice like an annoying wind blowing through a bad sinus condition whined at Alice, "Who gave you permission to sit at my desk?"

Alice pulled her head up and found herself staring straight into the face of a blue-eyed rabbit chewing gum, who blew a large bubble in her face. "I'm sorry, I thought it was my desk."

"You thought wrong. Now get out of my chair. And don't let it happen again. Paper processors don't have desks. They are much too busy to sit." Alice moved quickly to the other side.

"Excuse me, but who are you?" Alice asked.

"I am Nick's personal assistant," she said. The fur on her head fell in a whirlwind of messy bits to her shoulders.

Alice, hoping to bridge some of the social gap between them, cleared her throat and said, "The hair, er, fur on your head is a most unusual color. What color would you say that is?"

"Raspberry. Sorta raspberry," she said, snapping her gum.

Alice thought, *It looks like she combs it with an egg beater.* As if to confirm this, the rabbit popped out a toy egg beater and ran it fore and aft through the raspberry fields right down to the black roots. From her desk she then extracted a bottle of nail polish that matched her hair and proceeded to polish the nails on each front paw.

Alice cleared her throat and extended her hand and said, "My name is Alice."

The rabbit ignored Alice's hand and blew on the raspberry nail. "Bunnifur Rarebit," she said.

"What do you do as a personal assistant to the rabbit?"

"I personally assist in getting his doing done. He's very busy and needs lots of help," she said, blowing on another nail.

Alice's mouth hung open and she stared for a moment and then said, "Well, he certainly hops around a lot."

Bunnifur's blue eyes took on a hot gleam. "You best shut your mouth and get your doing done before Nick gets back," she said. Her phone rang. "Oh Mumsey, I got the most beautiful nail polish. And go to that purse website I told you about. I'm ordering a new one now." She clicked some keys on her computer and pulled out her credit card for some purse shopping.

She's a rare bit all right, Alice thought. She set about alphabetizing five shelves of binders and filing loose papers in the filing cabinets that sat along the scratched walls like fat tin soldiers. *The drawers roll out at me like swollen nasty tongues*, she thought. She found a ladder and moved other binders that were dusty and (she presumed) infrequently used to a high shelf. The whole time Alice worked, Bunnifur talked on the phone to Mumsey, giving her a running commentary of her online shopping selections. Alice speculated that maybe Bunnifer's rabbit species had a lazy-ass gene.

Nick hopped back into the pit straight over to Bunnifur's desk. He twitched his ears against hers and put a paw around her shoulders. "Bunny, dear, were there any messages while I was gone?"

"I've been much too busy. I let them go to voice mail. I'll check them later after my break." She pulled her purse from a drawer and sauntered off out of the pit.

"Oh, well yes, I know how busy you are, Buns." Turning to Alice, he said, " You can take a page from Bunny's book; she knows how to get doing done."

"If you mean she polishes her nails, talks to her mother, combs her hair, chews gum, and shops online, she does that a lot," Alice replied sarcastically.

The rabbit ignored her and began squeaking as if his tie was pulled too tight at his neck. She stood quietly, supposing eventually he'd let her know why he was so excited.

"This stack," he told her, "is too high. Too high." He pointed to the dusty binders. How can you expect me to reach it? Throw this group of binders away," he said, pointing to the five shelves she'd just alphabetized. And"—he extracted a large file with a furry paw—"this was to have been sent to the duchess last week."

"I wasn't even here last week. How can I possibly know those other things. You did not tell me. Though I distinctly remember saying—"

"Oh, worry and bother," the rabbit interrupted. "Send that file to the duchess immediately. She will rightsize you, you know, if she finds out it was your mistake."

"Rightsize? What does that mean? How can she make me a different size when I am the size I am? And how can it be my mistake when I wasn't even here to make it? We could have saved ourselves all this worry and bother—"

The rabbit interrupted, twisting his paws, "Oh, worry

and bother. I am late. I am late. Late for a meeting. Do I have to tell you everything? The duchess is the vice president of rightsizing. She can restructure anyone into any size she wants."

Alice squirmed inside at the prospect of someone able to restructure her into any size other than the one she was. But then she remembered her time during the reign of Prince Executive Charming. See the prince in Technicolor and bold print. See the prince dress Alice in navy-blue and white. See Alice be quiet, make a good impression, and not make waves. See Alice make herself very small to make the prince seem even larger still. In a way she was quite familiar with the concept. There it was called marriage; here it was called rightsizing. Some things were the same, no matter where you went.

"Use your head. Use your head. Get that file to the duchess. I am late," Nick said. In a flash he faded beyond the paper stacks in a double-timed hop.

"It will mostly be my hands I'll have to use," she said, but mostly to herself. She found an envelope and printed in large neat letters "To the Duchess, Vice President of Rightsizing. Delivery due last week," and began walking in the direction of the rabbit's back. She hoped to meet someone who knew the way. Asking Lenny the Lizard was not an option. His bleeping tongue flicks made her feel like scrubbing in a long hot shower.

A very long hallway traveled out of the other side of the pit. Waves of gray, from almost black at the pit side to pale white-gray at the other end, ranged the length of the hall. The shadings repeated themselves on the ceiling overhead and the floor below. The waves made

Alice feel she was being propelled along and would be spit out at the other end.

At the other end was a very old toad who limply held up splayed fingers as if this was the most physical exertion he'd experienced in days. "Halt," he said. He sat at a black half-circle desk slowly tapping a pencil on a clipboard with his other hand. Flowing black letters stitched above the breast pocket on his blue shirt read Old Guard.

His eyes were large and dull, and his skin was quite bleached and pasty, as if he'd been working underground too long. She thought he might be sensitive to the sun and sunburn easily. He was very old and probably ill and didn't appear to be the sharpest pencil in the desk. Nevertheless, he was the only one she could ask. "Could you help me, sir?"

"I'm very busy," he croaked. He coughed the words out in gray puffs as if smoking them.

"It doesn't look like you are doing anything," Alice said.

"I sit here for days and days and by and by I have something to do. I am an old retainer, sitting here till I retire. I do not want my schedule interrupted." Gray flakes sloughed off his face to his shoulders. His large eyes kept looking at the ceiling.

Alice thought this very rude. *But perhaps*, she thought, *he really can't help it. And one should respect the elderly and infirm, and maybe it has something to do with his skin condition.* In her past Cinderella life, she had been used to whitewashing everyone else's behavior. It seemed she was always wrong and everyone else was always right, so excusing their behavior somehow made her feel right. Instead of objecting to his behavior, she said, "The duchess was expecting this last week, and we need to get it to her or we will all be rightsized."

"Why didn't you say so?" he said. He jumped up and grabbed the file. The clipboard clattered to the floor. In two seconds he swung open the floor-to-ceiling double doors next to his desk and leaped through to the other side. Alice briefly wondered about the specter of the duchess, whose very name jumpstarted old toads and clocked frightened rabbits at twice their normal speed.

She hurried back to the pit. She feverishly pulled papers out and stacked them in drawers, files, and neat boxes, clearing an area nearest to Nick's office to show him her progress. Lenny and his bleeping forklift arrived and dumped an even bigger stack of boxes in the same spot, blocking Nick's office door. Her heart dropped to the floor. It looked like she'd accomplished nothing.

Just at that moment, Nick hopped back into the pit, squeaking, "What have you been doing while I've been gone? Nothing, it seems. It's worse than before. I can't even get in my office door."

Alice sputtered and felt her face getting very red. "But, but I—"

"But nothing. You've done nothing. What I've asked is very simple—to organize a few pieces of paper."

Alice rolled her eyes over the cavernous paper pit. "A few pieces of paper," she muttered under her breath and squelched the urge to scream. "Lenny keeps dumping more in the pit. Why, the paper multiplies like rabbits," she said, and then gulped when she realized what she had just said.

Nick squealed, "What did you just say?"

Alice got very red in the face. Her voice trailed off to a whisper, "There is so much paper it seems to multiply like, er, rabbits, sir."

"Are you making fun of my species?"

"Oh, no. I wouldn't do that, sir."

"See that you don't, or I will have to report you for discrimination against my species. I'll let it go this time. But remember, I have the PhD in management. I know best." He pointed at Alice. "I want the boxes away from my door ASAP."

Alice fumed. She was steamed. *He and the lizard act in the most inappropriate manner,* she thought, *and that is acceptable, but one teensy little slip of the tongue and they threaten to report me.* She would have loved to report the bleeping rabbit and the bleeping lizard. She grabbed a hand cart and slammed it under the stack of offending boxes. She cleared the area to Nick's office door while he pointedly stared and impatiently tapped his wing-tip shoe. He walked in and slammed the door without a thank-you, good job, or have a nice day. She smiled grimly over having a nice day. She doubted he ever did have a nice day, much less wish that anyone else would.

Alice clenched her teeth to hold in four-letter words. The prince had always known best. Now the rabbit knew best. Alice's best was her worst, according to both of them. She wanted to get out of here, but she had a creeping feeling that the rabbit was not going to let her go no matter how hard she worked. Meanwhile, she would do the rabbit's bidding and look for the first chance to escape.

She stacked. She filed. She shredded, once again

clearing the whole area around Nick Rabbit's office and even to the next supporting pillar and beyond. She wiped her brow with her scarf. She moaned. This was just like housework only on a bigger scale. No matter how much she did, she had to do the same thing all over again. And she never got finished.

The phone on Bunnifur's desk rang an annoying ring like it was belching computer chips.

Nick yelled from his office, "Answer that. Don't you know anything? You are to answer Bunnifur's phone when she is on a break."

"I'm sorry, I didn't know, " Alice said.

"It's in your job description," the Rabbit said curtly.

"When do I get a break like the Bunnifer?"

"Paper processors don't get breaks, which is also in your job description," the Rabbit shouted.

She clenched her teeth and bunched her fists at her sides. "A job description I've never seen, I might add," she shouted back.

He ignored her and yelled, "Just answer the phone."

Alice unclenched her teeth and fists and tried to answer in a courteous voice, "Mr. Nick Rabbit's office."

A shrill voice shrieked in Alice's ear. "It's me. Tell the rabbit I want it *now*."

Alice cleared her throat and politely asked, "Who can I say is calling?" Then she held the phone a safe distance from her ear.

"The rabbit knows," the voice yelled, and the receiver slammed in her ear before Alice could respond.

Nick stood just inside his opened door. His shaking paw rattled the knob. "That was the duchess, wasn't it?"

"She didn't say who she was," Alice said.

"What did she want?"

"She didn't say, but she wants it now. How confusing and rude, not to tell someone who you are or what you want and expect them to give it to you right away."

"That was the duchess," Nick said. He combed his whiskers with his fingers. "You know nothing about business."

"But," she asked, "how can you ever tell what she wants?"

"How do you know how to do your job?" he countered.

"Well, mostly I don't. Somehow things get done, but nothing ever gets finished."

"There, you see, it gets done."

Alice said, "Just because you're moving doesn't necessarily mean you're making any progress."

"You know nothing about business. Doing is progress. Getting doing done is business," he said, puffing out his chest. "I taught mismanagement at Old Misalliance University before I came here."

"It does seem you certainly learned what you taught," Alice mumbled under her breath. Then in a louder voice, she said, "I have a suggestion." She rather hoped this would make a favorable impression on the rabbit and get her out of here sooner.

He puffed up his chest fur and looked down his stubby nose at Alice, who was bent over a paper stack, and said, "I doubt someone with your inexperience and lack of education would have one, but what is it?"

"Get a BlackBerry. You'd always be connected. You'd know immediately when the duchess calls even when you are hopping around," Alice pointed out. "The prince had one, and he was connected 24/7. He was more married to it than to me," she added, but she thought *I wouldn't want to be married to either one.*

His ears drooped. His fur vibrated in a furious shaking. "Oh, worry and bother. That would never do." He shook his head as if to clear the vision of a closer connection to the duchess. He discharged a breath. His ears flipped back up. "And besides, it is recognized that my species is paw-challenged. Yes, we are paw-challenged," he repeated as if the thought was a duchess antidote, "and are exempt from BlackBerry use." One paw pounded his chest and his throat emitted a large burp that traveled out his rabbity lips and smelled like rancid carrot soup.

"You're not paid to ask questions *or* offer suggestions. That's why I am the esteemed director of paper processing, PhD, and you are the generic paper clerk number ten." He stood inches from her body, eyes on her breasts. A pool of saliva collected at the corner of his mouth. "Your bumps ... your bumps are very large."

"My bumps. My bumps," she stammered.

"No. No. You misunderstand," he said, wiping the corner of his mouth with his sleeve. "Your bundles, your bundles of paper are very large. Can I help you carry these?"

"Mr. Nick Rabbit," she said, "My eyes are up here. I would prefer you look at them when we talk."

"Oh, no, you misunderstand. You misunderstand. You see, I am a vertically challenged person. I can't help it. Can't help it that my eyes are on the same level as your bumps … er … ah, chest. It is not my problem that you are tall. Actually it would be more respectful to my stature if you would dip your knee to bring us eye level to eye level. See, you can correct this problem you are having by just dipping your knees."

How ridiculous, she inwardly fumed. Her knees locked. Her mouth got dry. Her face flashed hot.

He handed her a sheet of paper. "This is what the duchess wants. Send this to the duchess immediately."

Alice dipped her knee. It twitched in a nearly uncontrollable urge to send Nick a knee-mail. "No problem, Nick," she said. She looked at the sheet of paper. At the top of the page she read Hot Tits in large block letters.

She gasped, jabbing at the offending letters. "What is this?"

His ears flushed a deeper pink. "Um, oh, well, yes, you see. That is not what you think. No indeed. No indeed. My paws slipped on the keys. As I said, I am paw-challenged. The whole word is Hot Litter. That's how we refer to confidential papers in Corporateland. Hot litter is confidential paper to be shredded. Not meant at all for the duchess. No indeed. Glad you noticed this. Just shred the Hot Hooters … er … Hot Ti … er. Just shred that paper."

She sucked in a reply, clenched her teeth around it, and tore the offending words into strips and the strips into confetti.

He then perched one foot on a stack of paper and the other on the floor in a wide *V* up to his crotch. Alice's jaw dropped open. She could see the outline of his tighty whiteys and what was underneath. He said, "I'm adding paper reproducer to your job description." She closed her mouth. He was an animal, after all, she reasoned, and unused to wearing clothes. Maybe his legs just needed a good airing. She wondered, *Is this only strange and embarrassing to me because I'm human?* She dropped her head to hide her flushed cheeks and couldn't even speak.

She cringed when she heard the approaching bleep of the forklift.

"Lenny, put the pallet there," the Rabbit said, pointing to the space Alice had just cleared.

"Alice, make one hundred copies each of the computer procedure binders and file in the stacks," demanded the rabbit.

Alice moaned. *God, how many binders were there?* "There must be at least one hundred binders," she said.

"One thousand to be exact," said the rabbit.

"Wouldn't it save time and space and money to file one copy on the computer and one on the shelf and then make copies on request?"

"I don't trust those computers. If it erases everything, then I'll be the hero because I have 100,000 hard copies."

"When shall I do it? I'm so busy with filing and stacking, I ... I ..."

"Now, now," he interrupted, "remember our policy of doing and leaving the thinking to me?"

"But, but—" she sputtered.

"If, and it's big *if,* you complete this, I'll see that you get a two-cents-an-hour raise."

"But I'm getting paid nothing now."

"There you go, a raise, just like I said."

"Why don't you hire a couple of *temporary* paper reproducers and give them the two cents an hour? Or Bunny Rarebit could help. They could concentrate on nothing but that and get it done quickly and I could continue organizing and filing."

"It's not in Bunny's job description. Assisting me is much too important. She is far too busy. You will have to manage without paper reproducers," he said. "The trouble with you is that you try to use your head too much and think. All you have to do is work harder. Faster. Remember, I'm always right except for that one single case when I was wrong."

Alice's voice rose to just below a shriek. "Who do you think you are to be telling me how to do this job? You are never here to see what I've done. You are always busy hopping off someplace. I've been working hard with no break. Bunnifur is on a permanent break and has an intimate relationship with her hair and nails and phone calls to Mumsey and does nothing but chew gum and ignore the ringing phone and take breaks and shop online. And you come in here dangling your degrees and tell me to work harder. Faster. Hard work doesn't get me anything at all except more hard work. And further, put a zipper on your salivating mouth and a bungee cord around your legs, or I'll send a knee-mail straight into the rabbit family jewels."

"Well, no need to get puffy," the rabbit said, trembling. He inched slowly away.

"Puffy!" Alice screamed. "Puffy? I'm steamed." But

she said it to the rabbit's back as he sped down a row of paper stacks. She collapsed in a heap. "Paper. If I see any more paper, I swear I'll find some matches and use them on this pit." Alice sat on a paper stack and pulled her knees to her chest. Two great droplets of water rushed down her cheeks. She sobbed such large, saucer-sized tears that they turned her sweater and scarf soggy and threatened to spill off the hem of her skirt and turn the paper around her into a pulpy mess. She broke out in a panicky cold sweat. *Out. I've got to get out of here! There has to be some way out.* She grabbed both arms around her middle and gave herself a good shake. *If anyone is going to get me out of here, it's me. I got myself out of once-upon-a-time with the prince when it turned unhappily ever after, and I can get myself out of here too. The trusting-the-Nick-Rabbit boat out of here sailed the moment I fell into the pit,* she thought. As suddenly as her tears had started, they stopped. She sat up, wiped each cheek with an arm, and fluffed her hair. She blew her nose on a crumpled sheet, shook herself out, and smoothed her rumpled skirt and sweater.

Out of the Pit

She peered around the paper stacks. Lenny the Bleeping Lizard was rounding the corner five rows down. She turned and sprinted on shaky knees in the opposite direction. All she had to do was make it to the other end and out the hallway past the old toad.

The bleeping grew louder. Over her shoulder, she saw Lenny turn down her aisle. Alice ran harder. She put leather to the cement, yanked up her skirt, and ran. She felt the prongs of the forklift hot on her heels.

"Stop," he yelled above the bleeping. "Running through the paper stacks is inappropriate behavior." She leveraged an arm on the shelving to steer around the corner. Lenny cut the same corner sharply and two-wheeled it after her. She whirled around and stopped, arms punched at her sides. He jammed the brakes. The prongs stopped within an inch of her knees.

"I will report this inappropriate behavior and unauthorized use of a break to U Nick." He dragged his tongue along his teeth and let it hang.

That revolting tongue, Alice thought as it began its

incessant flick. *What if I were to grab hold and yank it?* Could she? Would she? Did she dare? What did she have to loose? "I'll show you inappropriate and unauthorized," she yelled. She strode to the side of the forklift, stuck her face in front of his pointed one, clenched her fist around his flicking tongue, and said, "Unless you keep your tongue in your head, I'll yank it out and feed it to the old toad at the end of the hallway. I'll tell him it's a juicy earthworm. Now I suggest you go slither under a dark paper stack someplace, if you can't find a rock."

"Ack. Ack. Gurgle. Ack," he gargled at the back of his throat. His eyes bulged. One hand massaged his throat while the other slowly twisted the steering wheel. Alice stepped with each turn. When he aimed the forklift the other way, she let go. His purple tongue slapped his face like a wet noodle.

"As for my unauthorized break, I haven't had one since I came here. I just authorized myself a permanent one. I am leaving this pit." With that, she shot her right arm straight up from the elbow, all fingers extended. "That's a whole handful of middle digits, Lenny. Take a handful to bleeping U Nick too," she yelled after the forklift speeding away in a puff of paper dust. He never looked back and neither did Alice.

Hammer. Hammer. Thud. Thud. Knock. She clutched her dress at her chest and tried to still her heart, which was about to pop through. She walked on legs like rubber down the waves-of-gray hall to the old toad's desk. She was grateful he was snoring into his clipboard. The snore was more like the bleat of a sheep with a cold and rattled the pen against the metal clipboard. She tiptoed past and pushed one of the double black doors. It squeaked.

The toad croaked midbleat, lifted his head slightly, and let it fall with a thunk back to the clipboard. Her heart pounded in her throat. She pushed the door slightly to open a small crack she could *just* slide through. It squeaked again, so loud that it reverberated across the hall, gaining volume that could have raised the dead—or a sleeping toad.

He snorted once into his clip board and jerked his head up. "Halt. Halt, I say. Thought you could get by my door alarm, did you?"

Alice thought quickly as she approached his desk. "I'm taking a message to the duchess for the rabbit."

"Where is it?" he coughed, rattling his clip board.

Alice tossed her head, "It's a verbal message. I'm to give it directly to the duchess."

He checked his clipboard. "You are not authorized to deliver messages to the duchess."

Alice began inching away toward the double doors.

"Halt, I say," he croaked. He splayed one foot on top of his desk and hopped over in one hop. The rough pads on his toes grasped her wrist like a handcuff. For such a weak-looking old toad, he was very strong. He began dragging her back toward the desk. She dug her feet into the carpet till the heat came through her heels. He halted so abruptly that it very nearly toppled them both to the floor. Her feet pounded the floor in place like a jogger waiting for a green light. Inch by inch she hauled him toward the double doors.

"Let me go," Alice said, trying to unpeel the pads of his toes from her wrist.

"The rabbit did not authorize you to leave the pit."

She breathed into his pointy face. "He can manage without me," she said. Her other hand reached up and gripped his tie by the knot at his throat. His toady eyes bulged.

"We have a problem we can both solve."

He croaked, "Gurgle, what, gurgle, problem?"

"I want to get out of here, and you want me to stop twisting your tie." She twisted it tighter. His eyes turned glassy and his knees crumpled and his toes released her fist as he fell to the floor. She released the tie from her fist and gasped. "Oh my God, I've killed the toad." She pushed the double doors wide open.

On the other side was a short hall with a set of elevators and a large arrow pointing at a black button with the words "You Are Here. Paper Pit." Another button had a large red arrow that said This Way Up. Alice ran the short distance and punched the red arrow. A whirring announced the arrival of an elevator. Alice looked back at the double doors. She was stunned. She thought she had killed the toad, but here he was, running toward her with his toes doing little wrist flaps at his side in rhythm with his croaky voice. "Rabbit cannot manage without her. Rabbit cannot manage without her."

If the elevator can just manage to get here before the toad does, she thought. And there it was. But there he was too, within a hop of grabbing for her wrist when the door slid open. Alice jumped inside and jabbed the close-door button.

The doors slid shut against his croaky voice. "He cannot manage without her. He cannot manage without her." As she ascended, she heard the faint pounding of his toes against the shut door below.

She wrapped her arms about her ribs to ensure she would not go spilling all over the floor. She felt herself unraveling, and that would never do if she was going to get out of here.

The elevator whirred. She didn't do anything. It seemed to know where it was going. The only way was up. Her heart settled to a more sedate rate. A panel of lighted words blinked on and off as she ascended: Paper Pit. Substandard Basement. Baseless Debasement. Off Basement. Lower than Low Lobby. Lower Lower Lobby. Lower Higher Lobby. Upper Snobby Lobby. Training Track. And with that the names stopped and so did the elevator as the doors opened and spit her out.

The Training Track

The doors opened on a gray mist that emanated from a gray hallway. Materializing from the fog and extending a wing to her, a very large bird said, "Grand Dodo Bird." The elevator doors slid shut. The tassels on his loafers jumped as he swaggered toward her.

She tipped her head back to get a good look up at his large hooked beak. *Well, I can certainly see that he is large*, Alice thought, but to call oneself grand did seem a bit pompous. She let her eyes drop to the navy-blue vest gapping at the buttons. He kept tugging at the bottom with his wing tips to keep it pulled over his plump middle.

He let go of his vest with one wing and moved it to his head. He smoothed a group of feathers up and over to one side of his head to cover the molting spot on the top that some birds get when they get older. The feathers had a life of their own and kept falling back to the original side. Unfortunately, this made the sides uneven.

Alice tried hard not to look at the feathers on each side, one above the ear and one falling toward the shoulder, or the molting spot on the top. *Maybe he has a self-image problem because he's at an evolutionary dead end*, she thought. She knew she'd been staring for longer than was polite when he cleared his throat. She checked a giggle in her throat.

"I am Grand Dodo Bird, the Corporateland trainer. Everybody calls me DB. Come work for me. Teamwork's my name. Teamwork's my game." He shot one wing straight up while the other wing clenched the top feathers from flipping over and exposing the bald spot. He yelled, "Yay, team. We're a team. We touch all biases here."

She shrank back and said, "Oh, so did the rabbit and the lizard. They were always doing and saying the most inappropriate things."

"No, you misunderstand. No, we truly value everyone here regardless of gender or animal orientation. We touch all bases here. Yay, team."

She let out the deep breath she'd been holding. "*Bases*, you mean *bases*. What a relief. I thought you said touch all biases."

"'Bases. Biases. Bases. Biases. We touch them all. Yay, team. And an added perk is you get out of the pit."

"No, you misunderstand. I don't want to stay here. I just want to get out. If you'll just point the way. Throw in a few lefts and rights or a north or south or two and I'll be on my way."

"The only way out is through the training track, and we will develop you beyond your expectations."

"My only expectations are to get out of here."

"You'll get training, of course. This is a training department. Training's my name. Training's my game.

Yay, team! You'll start off as a generic word processor with lots of room to develop you past your expectations. But later. We'll discuss details later."

Alice raised her voice to practically a shout. "I just want out. O-U-T. Out."

The dodo fluffed his feathers and thumbed a file under his wing, completely ignoring what she'd said. "Yes, we will discuss your training later. Now I am about to conduct a training session for the new management team. Come and observe. I want you to feel the spirit, feel a part of the team. Yay, team!"

Before Alice could make another plea for directions out, a disembodied voice came over a crackling speaker system and solemnly intoned a sort of prayer. DB stopped and quickly slapped a feathered wing over his heart.

I pledge allegiance to you, your Highness,
Who art in Corporateland.
Hallowed is thy game.
Hallowed is thy name.
Give us this day the salaries to buy our daily bread
And lead us not into the temptation of saying
otherwise, lest we lose our daily bread.
Yea though I walk through the Valley of the Shadow of
Losing my Job,
It comforts me to see you see clearly while we are all in
the dark.
Your word is first, last, and always until your next
word becomes first, last, and always.
If you say it is so, it is so.

You have the power seldom to be what you represent
yourself to be.
For thine is the kingdom, and the glory, and the power
and manipulation and five-hundred-million-dollar
salary and stock options and bonuses forever and ever.

"What on earth was that?" Alice asked.

"Every morning his Highness's pledge is broadcast to everyone," the Dodo replied, "to remind us who butters our bread."

"Sounds like that means he can say what he wants without setting a good example," Alice said.

"Of course. His Highness doesn't have to stand on his words, because he walks on everyone else's. That's why he was elected the crowned executive omnipotent." With that, the Dodo returned his wing to his side. He grabbed Alice's arm.

"But if you would be so kind, Mr. Grand Dodo Bird, as to just …"

He turned, clamped a wing over her arm, and dragged her after him, saying, "No more discussion until after the training session is over."

Alice decided maybe the most direct way out was an indirect cooperative one as he practically lugged her across the hall from the elevator to a spinning revolving door. No one pushed it. Round and round it went without anyone in it. Alice bobbed her head in circles, mesmerized by this door that had a life of its own. Dodo Bird shoved her into a slot and stepped into his own slot on the next spin. He stepped off into the large room on the other side. Alice ran along inside the door to keep up with its spin, but she couldn't maneuver the stepping-off part. Each time she passed the Dodo Bird, she mouthed through the glass, "How do I get off?" Her words got distorted by the fast spinning and came out one word per spin.

The bird pushed something on the wall next to the door, and mechanical arms cupped her rear and ejected her into his plump middle. "Oof," he breathed and checked his feather alignment.

"Why does the door keep spinning? Why can't it be pushed at everyone's own speed?" she asked, brushing her hands down her sweater and skirt.

"It's a management training exercise. At least one point in everyone's career, if not more, they will all assume a revolving-door-management role. We hold them in temporary positions until someone decides what to do with them. Sometimes they keep spinning in place, and sometimes they are unexpectedly ejected. We train them in all phases of management."

"It must be very disorienting and frustrating to keep spinning and accomplish nothing," she said.

"It teaches them to expect the unexpected. We're very thorough in our training."

They entered a large circular room about the size of a gymnasium. In the center was a milling herd of giraffes. All had BlackBerrys clutched awkwardly in their hooves and were punching with a frenzy at the tiny keyboards. Alice felt vindicated in her suggestion to the rabbit. This species used BlackBerrys even though they were hoof-challenged.

"His Highness is mentoring this new crop of giraffes," the bird told Alice as they walked across the parquet floor. "He wants to leave a living legacy when he retires in a few years. He is a giraffe himself, you know. Larger than life. They are not as large as life now, but if they just follow his hoof prints, they too can attain his stature.

It's rumored that he will pay a surprise visit to this training session to deliver his famous truth sermon." He raised a wing like he was swearing on a Bible. "An oral injection of the truth, the whole truth, and nothing but the truth, so help me Corporateland."

Goodness, Alice thought, *this sounds like a religious experience. Maybe there will be some great enlightenment to show me the way out of here.*

The very next moment, all giraffe heads swiveled in the direction of the revolving door. A gasp whooshed up the neck of each giraffe with such velocity that it created quite a stir of air. It was an audience of open-mouthed amazement. Hooves halted midtype on their BlackBerrys as the giraffes quickly tucked them in breast pockets.

Alice and the Dodo Bird swiveled too, toward a giant giraffe striding through the door, which stopped mid-revolution as the partitions parted. He was taller still from his upright stance on hind hooves. Mirror-polished wing-tip shoes shined on each hind hoof. Front hooves and legs swung from his side like arms. He flowed onto the scene like slick, smooth acrylic swabbed onto a canvas in broad strokes. A simple crown in tasteful hammered gold adorned his head. It clung regally to the horns on top.

"The crowned executive omnipotent," the giraffes intoned in unison. Alice shrank back against the wall and then slowly unpeeled herself when she realized no one was paying the slightest bit of attention to her. She kept a respectful distance from the giraffe's thin legs, which promised a potent kick despite the trousers he wore.

With an inclined reverential head, the grand dodo said, "What an honor, your Highness, to grace us with your presence."

"Yes, well, isn't it? I was just saying to Bill—you know Bill—no, no, of course you don't know Bill. He being farther up in the Big House and you down here at the training track. I was just saying to Bill, I need to stay in touch with the new crop of giraffes." He snapped his front hooves together sharply, which was apparently some kind of summons.

A door labeled Imaging Center slid open behind him. Three pony-tailed, jeans-clad fish scissor-stepped across the floor, pushing dollies with cameras. They hopped into hydraulic sky buckets and positioned the cameras in front and on both sides of the CEO for an intimate head shot. He aimed two more hoof snaps at the fish with the side cameras. They gulped, looked worried and remorseful as if they'd made a mistake, and maneuvered quickly to the front on either side of the fish with the front camera.

Alice saw immediately why and drew in a surprised breath. Quite involuntarily, she said, "Why, you are as thin as a playing card from the side. It's only if I move in front of you that you are 3-D and in Technicolor. There's no apparent substance to you from the side. You are like a sheet of paper." As if to demonstrate, she moved from side to front several times and then stopped directly in front of him and craned her head up.

He looked down a long inclined neck at Alice and said, "Who is this human? I don't recall approving a human in this training session. DB, I'm sure we had our quota of humans in the last session."

Wringing his wings, he said, "Quite right, your Highness. She is here for the word processing position. I invited her to observe."

"Oh, yes. I have observed that human females make excellent word processors. Smart move, DB. Pretty little thing too, for a human. But it is clear her view is not clear. She is not familiar with our imaging center's hollow graphic technology. She may stay, but only if she watches my hollow graphic image from the front. Otherwise, have her removed," he said, biting off "removed" through tight teeth. Alice shrank back, slipped behind a camera dolly out of view, and when the CEO wasn't watching, peeked out from behind.

He dressed his face in professional pleasantness for

the cameras. The look registered somewhere between a smile and a wince. His long navy-blue silk tie dotted with large white polka dots flowed from the base of his long thick neck. A matching silk handkerchief flopped from his jacket breast pocket. He smoothed the tie, which didn't need smoothing, and reflopped the handkerchief in a practiced study of casual correctness. His silk tie and scarf were of such fresh, tasteful elegance it was as if they had been snatched from the jaws of Japanese silkworms just finished spinning.

All the trainees wore the same outfit, down to the navy double-breasted suit with the deep red pinstripe. There were two notable exceptions: they were still in training suits, which allowed for a four-legged stance, whereas the CEO stood upright. And the trainees dressed in off-the-rack polyester and faux silk while the CEO was arrayed in Italian tailored wool.

He pranced. He danced toward them in a smooth foxtrot till he stopped in front of them, so close that they all bent backward to look up. The fish crew quickly swung sky buckets front and center to keep pace with him.

Alice noticed one albino with pale beige markings and pink eyes. Her hooves were altered, molded, and shaved to produce a high-heeled spike on all four hooves. She tottered at the ankles, slightly off-balance. "Excuse me, your Highness," said Alice. "Why aren't there more albino giraffes?"

His Highness swung his neck back toward Alice, and through clenched teeth, he said, "You clearly can't keep your opinions to yourself, but in this case, your comment offers a prime example of our diversity program." He blew on an upraised hoof and buffed it across his jacket. "My idea, I might add."

"How can it be diverse when there is only one that is different?" Alice said. "Why can't there be more albinos and more women giraffes so it's balanced?"

"She is our token Blanco."

"A token what?"

"A token Blanco to demonstrate racial and gender diversity. That's what token means: superficial evidence that my program is working. And efficient on our part, I might add, to fulfill racial and gender diversity in one giraffe." He flicked a hoof at Alice and pointed to the space behind the camera dolly.

Alice was speechless. What a bunch of horse apples, as her grandfather used to say, but she tightened her lips against any further reply. His hoof flicks looked like they could carry a painful kick.

He raised a hoof at the dodo's offer of a podium. "I shall address the troops with no barriers in an open demonstration of openness. We shall talk giraffe to giraffe. Mind you, all—I say *all*—animals are to be respected regardless of genetics, racial slurs, or sexual disorientation."

Alice knew she was not supposed to speak, but she thought if she were helpful, he might view her more favorably. She inched out from behind the dolly, cupped her hands, and sent a loud whisper up his long neck to an ear. "Psst, your Highness. I'm just trying to be helpful, your Highness, sir. I'm sorry to interrupt, but shouldn't it be gender, race, or animal orientation?"

Flicking her whisper away like annoying flies buzzing around his head he said, "Yes. Yes. That's what I said; everyone's to be respected because of all that stuff. Giraffes are not more equal despite their imposing stature. We put our pants on one, two legs at a time. Well, in the trainees' case, until they have gained my stature, they put theirs on one, two, three, four legs at a time. We must be tolerant of others who cannot help the afflictions they were born with. I tolerate everyone, till they become intolerable.

"Why, I was talking on the phone two weeks ago with Willie Simpleton. Giraffe to Simpleton. It was I who filled his campaign coffers to get him elected head of the states. Stole all the bases he did. Now, unfortunately, he can't hit the ball unless that wife of his is involved." At that he pulled a front hoof to his mouth and gnawed.

"And what does he do after he's elected? Turns over the nationwide problem of national paper pallet delivery to every backyard to his wife." He spit the word *wife* and pieces of hoof through his tight lips. His long, curly lashes bunched as he squeezed his eyes shut. "Now if she does call to consult with me, don't know whether I'll talk to the little woman or not. Dabbling her legal eagle feathers in paper production without consulting me. Her uninformed reform could seriously impede my paper pallet production. He stamped back to the podium and pounded the gnawed hoof on the wood. "I tell you, I will not have it!"

He paused, let his eyes remain briefly shuttered, and then snapped them open in a silent call to attention. He extracted a spotless white monogrammed handkerchief from his back pocket and deliberately, delicately dabbed the corners of his eyes. Each neck strained forward for his next words as if closer proximity would allow for greater absorption of meaning.

Alice nudged the cameraman and said in a loud whisper with her hands on her hips, "Did you hear that? Calling this prominent woman 'the little woman' like she's not a person with a name and a brain!"

His Highness whipped his long neck around toward Alice. "I didn't say you could speak."

Alice cleared her throat. "Excuse me, your Highness, I couldn't help myself. It sounded so disrespectful."

His Highness glared at DB. "Dodo, see that the human keeps her thoughts to herself or see that she is removed."

The thought of being removed before she found her way out kept Alice's mouth firmly shut. She hoped eventually she would hear something worth hearing. She bit her lips and pinched them together. This place was more and more like her time with the prince: she could be seen but not heard and above all must walk ten steps behind. *This is just a different branch of royalty*, she thought.

His Highness continued, head low, eyes magnetically fixed on each member of the audience in turn. Their heads followed with each turn of his. He and they were one smooth piece. "What will it profit a man if he gains another paper market but loses his own supply? Listen up. You are giraffe trainees now, but you too can be the top giraffe, shaving strokes off your best game, carrying the ball for the touchdown, slam dunking it for Corporateland. Remember we are biz biz, if you remember nothing else. We are out there busting our assets for the people of the world who do not have paper. Our sole purpose in Corporateland is to serve the people of the world with paper.

"I do want to acknowledge all that bad press about cutting down tree houses to make paper. Our technology department, as I speak, is now close to developing synthetic paper, a petroleum-based product that only uses old dead fossil fuel. And, I might add, drilling holes ventilates an overheated planet. It's a win-win situation."

Alice could not help herself. "Your Highness, I know you said I wasn't to speak, but this makes no sense at all. Drilling holes in the Earth won't cool off the planet. But more trees and more shade ..."

He bared his teeth at Alice. She shrank back behind the dolly. He continued, "No one wants to stop the cutting of the tree houses more than I. But it's lonely here at the top. I make tough, ambiguous contabulations to serve the world paper crisis. I go to bed each night gratified, satisfied, and beatified that I have served humanity in its moment of need.

"But I will not rest on our past assets when there are still people who do not have adequate supplies of paper to fill their in- and out-baskets. Their trays are empty. Indeed, they have *no* paper to print documents attached to e-mails. They sit idle at their desks. No paper to read. They are halted in their chairs. Esteem has plummeted. Heads have dipped to half mast, looking through their navels. The only view, their old assets. Some have been heard to mutter, 'Oh, excrement. Oh, excrement.'

"We have the power to change the view." With that his long neck snapped up and he stretched taller still on his hind legs, cameras following. "Our mission is world-class paper distribution. State-of-the-art delivery. We've purchased a fleet of small planes to fly low over Third World countries and the Pacific Rim to do paper drops and expand our markets. We're producing more paper for a better tomorrow. Remember your goal. My goal. Our goal: be so far ahead, we are just behind the next time."

Alice loudly cleared her throat and politely raised her hand. "Um, if you please, your Highness ..."

His Highness stomped his hoof and said, "Yes, yes, what is it now?"

"I just don't understand how a goal can be so far ahead that it's behind. Most respectfully, your Highness, sir, this doesn't make any sense."

His Highness ground his teeth and then spit out, "Dodo, reconsider that human you've just hired or the Duchess of Rightsizing may have to resize you."

Dodo gulped and tugged his head feathers. Alice retreated behind the camera.

His Highness cast one last bid-for-attention look over the sea of giraffe heads. His hoof stamped against the floor. Sky buckets retracted. Jeans-clad fish, cameras, sky buckets, and dollies rolled into the hole in the wall from which they'd come. He cantered backwards, hollow graphic image intact. The revolving door stopped its incessant spin. The glass partitions parted. The performance was over with no curtain calls. He flicked a crowned head back at them. "Carry on, Dodo." The training track roared with hooves applauding against the parquet floor.

"First," the dodo announced, "I'm going to mark a circle." His head feathers flopped away from his careful combing as he bent down to mark places for everyone in front of the doors of assorted shapes and sizes, about one hundred of them, that filled the wall around the circle. Each door had a large brass ornamental knob and a scrolled keyhole.

The grand dodo stood up and gave his head a quick snap. The feathers landed in their retrained places. All of a sudden, the giraffes started running around in the circle. He didn't even say "one, two, three, go." They craned their long necks down and back, eyes darting furtively from corner to corner, trying to see who was catching up to whom.

"Is this a game, Mr. Dodo? Are they pretending they are being chased by their natural predator? Or is this just for the incentive of running?"

The dodo said, "Watch and observe management training at its best." He called out to the giraffes, "The race is over, now select a door."

By and by some stopped, while others kept on. It was really difficult to tell who was winning.

Those remaining tried to turn the door knobs where they were standing, but they were all locked. Alice said, "If they are all locked, how will they get in?"

"*Are* they to get in at all? That is the question," the dodo said. "Risk takers make it. But don't make a mistake," he added with a sly glance.

"Could you identify a mistake?" Alice asked.

"They'll be told immediately after they make it," the dodo replied.

Alice pursed her lips. "If they don't know it ahead of time, how can it be a mistake?"

"Alice, all they have to remember are four important points regarding mistakes:

- Disavow any wrongdoing.
- Don't, under any circumstances, admit you made one.
- Blame it on someone else who was acting without your knowledge.
- And most important, remember mistakes are not tolerated, much less repeated.

"Then," he said, flourishing a wing and simultaneously opening one door, "if the mistake is repeated, they are assigned an empty desk in this empty office as part of the decruitment program until someone decides how to get rid of them."

All of a sudden, the floor on which the giraffes were standing started rumbling, undulating. At first, Alice thought it was an earthquake. Then the room turned into a series of side-by-side moving sidewalks from one side to the other. The whole room was like one giant treadmill test. Their hooves thundered on the conveyor belts as they ran in place to avoid a giraffe-to-wall head-on collision. The belts reversed direction several times. They ran backward. They ran forward. They ran sideways. They maintained their place. Sweat rolled down their long necks. Starched collars turned limp.

Breast-pocket handkerchiefs flopped in disarray. Heads bent down and bit the backs in front of them. Hooves kicked other hooves. Then abruptly the belt kicked into a high-speed blur. And they ran faster still, till each hoof was a dark spinning wheel. Through it all, they furiously punched on their BlackBerrys.

The dodo grabbed a microphone and flipped the volume to maximum decibels. His voice squawked over the thundering hooves. "You are now experiencing the work simulator." The simulator stopped as abruptly as it had started. Sweaty giraffe bodies tossed and rocked against each other on thin legs, trying to maintain an upright position. "Any questions?" the dodo asked. All stood panting beyond words.

Alice raised her hand timidly and cleared her throat. "I have one, Mr. Grand Dodo."

"Yes, yes. What is it?" he asked impatiently.

"Why were their feet spinning like little wheels?"

"Excellent question. Excellent question indeed. You have to learn to run that fast just to stay in the same place."

"How do they ever get any other place?" Alice asked.

"Why, they have to run twice as fast as that," he said smugly.

The trainees collapsed into a semi-circle in front of the grand trainer. Their panting had quieted to heavy breathing. Hooves shot in the air. Weary giraffe faces filled with questions.

"Before you ask any questions, I want to introduce you to the three-minute manager that answers all your questions on how to manage. There is a credit-card sized version in the front flap of your binders. Refer to it now. Refer to it often. When in doubt, read it. Repeat it. It's your personal manager mini-Bible. Yay, team."

With that, he stood solemnly, one wing crooked at his breast over his heart, while a Corporateland flag was unfurled from the ceiling till it waved just over their heads. The shiny black corporate seal flapped his flippers on a field of green currency in the center of the black flag. The bird's beak hinged open and shut over each word as if he were precisely chewing them. It was a sermon. It was divine liturgy. He was grave, his voice deep and hollow.

"Direct, but don't expect direction.

"Take risks, but don't make mistakes.

"We expect perfection.

"Demand. Control. Intimidate.

"Self-aggrandize. Probe. Berate.

"Drive change. Be committed.

"Do not be outwitted.

"When uncertain, when in doubt, run in circles, scream, and shout.

"Commit yourself till you feel you should be committed.

"Be open. Sensitive. Aggressive.

"Above all, strive to be obsessive.

"Give 30 percent to United Fund and blood on your lunch hour, drop by drop.

"'Tis better to give than receive, behold that thought.

"Donate five thousand dollars to the CEO's campaign chest.

"Dinner with the kids and wife?

"Above all, do what you think is best.

"But let me make this perfectly clear:

"Though we understand your free time is dear,

"It is strongly suggested that you volunteer at a soup kitchen from nine to one a.m.

"Go to bed. Wake up and do it all over again.

"I now pronounce you a member of management team. We are your corporate family. Your home away from home. I want you to know I have an open-door policy should there be anything you wish to discuss. I am a pathetic listener," he concluded as he strode over to the door labeled Grand Dodo Bird, Trainer, and slammed it behind him. A key turned and a lock clicked.

Alice stood with her mouth ajar. But no one else thought it odd to close and lock a door after an open-door policy speech. *Maybe they're all pathetic listeners.* She closed her mouth and watched them march out of the room. They shuffled binders and papers into fine leather cases with gold initials and combination locks. No one had opened a binder, though each was stamped with a picture of a seal on a rock slapping his flippers together, balancing a ball on his nose while juggling eight more. "Corporateland" was written in a half circle over his head. He sat on a pedestal stamped with the words Corporate Seal. Underneath, it read "Dedicated to Money and Mergers, Acquisitions and Rightsizing." Management Training 101 was printed in small letters in the lower right corner.

"Please exit through the revolving door," a recorded voice droned from a ceiling speaker. The giraffes tucked their necks and long legs into balls and leveraged themselves into door slots. One by one, the same mechanical hands that had pushed Alice into the room somersaulted them out into the hallway on the other side. She assumed that, anyway, having come in that way. The view out was obscured by clouded, opaque glass.

B.S. Session

First a degree-ridden dimwit of a rabbit, and now a pathetic listener in extinct dodo bird feathers. *I've got to get out*, Alice thought. Out. Of. Here. Now. She rapped her knuckles against the door. "Mr. Grand Dodo …"

"Yes, who is it?" she heard from the other side, rather like he had just taken a bite of food and was chewing and talking at the same time.

"It's Alice, Mr. Grand Dodo. You promised me after the training session you would show me the way out. If you will just give me the directions, I won't bother you any more. And could you use your open-door policy when you give me directions?"

"My open-door policy is closed now. I'm very busy," he said with a noisy slurping as if he was sucking something through a drinking straw. "And, Anita, as I told you when you got off the elevator, the only way out is through the training track," he said through more muffled chewing. "I need a yes or no answer or I shall ask the agency to send someone else."

Through clenched teeth she said, "Alice, my name

is Alice. There's been some mistake. I wasn't asking for a job. Well, I was originally. But after working for the rabbit, I can see I am not suited to this place. I just want out. Just point me at the proper door and I'll walk through it."

"Alma, yes or no? Do you want in or out?" he repeated.

"Alice, my name is Alice. Out," she said firmly, shoulders back, back straight. "Out of here."

Through more muffled chewing, he said, "You cannot pass go until you pass word processing."

"Are you quite sure?" she asked.

He smacked his beak and said, "Quite sure."

Alice's heart sank and threatened a descent all the way back to the paper pit. It was another no-win situation. Corporateland two, Alice zero. She sighed a sigh that was half hope and half reservation. *To be developed past one's expectations* is *intriguing*, she half-heartedly justified.

She was tired of standing at his door trying to talk through it. She slid down to the floor, leaned against the door, pulled her knees to her chest, and spoke to the crack, "What exactly is word processing?"

"It's the big T at the big C in the Big House."

She privately thought that if it sounded important, it was sure not to be, except to them.

"The what at the what?" she asked.

"Typing on a computer at Corporateland's headquarters," he replied. "Don't you know anything?"

"Not much, it seems. Until recently, all I knew was the paper pit, and then I had a past life as Prince Executive

Charming's wife, and then way before that I did learn typing in high school. Mother said I should learn it in case the prince died. But that was thirty years ago. Not since the prince died. Since I learned typing. Actually there wasn't even a prince then, when I learned typing; it was a just-in-case-thing when I married him. If he died. He didn't die, but the marriage did."

The dodo almost crowed. "There, you see, your mother was right."

"No, it means that typing and marriage were all I prepared myself to do. I suppose it would come back with some use," she said, flexing her fingers. Her heart jumped, a hopeful jump. It *was* a way out, and she'd get training in *something*, but her mind was doubtful.

"I'm in a head and feathers sort of a bind," said the dodo. "I'm flapping my wings a lot and not getting off the ground since my word processor left."

"Why did this person leave?"

"We developed her past her expectations. She went on to what she'd always dreamed of being, a personal assistant to his Highness Jr., otherwise known as the Golden Boy or GB for short. He's being groomed to replace his Highness, the crowned executive omnipotent, when he retires. Quite an important position."

"Quite important for him, at least," Alice said. "But does that make her important just because she works for him?" The answer was critical. Alice really wanted to know the answer to this question. The only way she'd felt important was being married to Prince Executive Charming. He was successful; therefore she was successful, as she was married to him. After climbing out of the prince-and-Alice fairy tale, she had landed in a giant paper pit, and she didn't want to leave her hopes forever in the heap of those two places. She didn't want to develop herself and fall into yet another pit. Still ...

She clenched her teeth. "Is it anything like management training?"

The dodo made more chomping noises and smacked his beak. "Oh, generic word processors are vastly *unimportant* compared to management. We hardly spend any time on them at all. Any dunce can do it. It's so easy. A program I developed, I might add."

She groaned, the lack of training with the rabbit fresh in her mind. She stood up and pounded loudly on the door. "Could you at least open the door and explain the training program to me?"

There was a long pause and some shuffling of papers, and then the lock clicked and the door opened just a crack. Feathers covered with crumbs slipped through the door toward Alice.

"Here, Abigail," he said. He wiped his beak with one wing and pushed a book at her with the other. Crumbs showered in all directions. Both wings retreated. He closed the door and clicked the lock.

"I thought you said I get training." Her words bounced off the door in front of her.

"Well, yes, Alana. You do," he said through the wood. "It's OJT in your DWA."

"Alice, my name is Alice," she said slowly, spitting the words between her teeth, her hands tight-fisted at her sides.

He brushed away her name like some of his sticky crumbs, saying, "Well, yes, whatever, Ann."

"Whatever is OJT and wherever is my DWA?" she countered.

"On the job training in your designated work area. Take the book to the desk across from my door. Begin at the start. Go on till you finish. Then stop. I am so excited. I am developing you beyond your expectations." He burped with such volume and vibration that the name plate rattled on the door. He smacked his beak and continued, "I won an award for this program for its cost-efficiency reduction in instructor hours. Training's my name. Training's my game. Yay, team."

Alice sighed again. Ever since she had arrived, she had felt compelled to do a lot of sighing, as if there wasn't enough oxygen in this weird place to sustain her, so she had to add extra inhalations and exhalations. She glanced down at the book, which was titled *Word Processing 101*. It was covered with crumbs and sticky feather prints.

She threw a despairing look at the desk against the wall, which was mounded with papers. A computer screen glared blankly at the papers stacked to the ceiling in the in basket. A ladder leaned against the stack for easy access to the top paper. The out-basket was empty. She gulped—her DWA, she supposed. *The in-basket should be shipped to the paper pit*, she thought.

The work area's only decoration was a picture of the CEO on the wall. A spotlight from the ceiling highlighted his gold crown, which was tipped at a rakish angle. His smile matched the self-satisfied whir of the revolving door. Both had hidden buttons with their own agenda.

Between the spinning door and her desk was a table hosting a platter of chocolate donuts, Styrofoam cups, creamer containers and sugar packets, and a tall steaming urn of coffee. She flipped the lever, let the coffee steam, and speared a donut over an index finger. She plunked herself down at the desk and began the dreary book on how to word process. Very soon, she finished one donut and began another, then another. The most curious thing happened. Her stomach got bigger and bigger; in fact, it got so large it looked as if she'd pulled a large inner tube over her head and was wearing it around her middle.

Oh my God, Alice thought. *What's causing this?* She'd only eaten a few donuts. Adding this many pounds and inches should not have happened that quickly. To test it out, she reached for a donut, and her waistline immediately started to expand. She pulled her hand back, and her stomach contracted. She picked up a donut, and she got bigger still. She moved it to her mouth and her waist reached the limits of her stretchy waistline. She put it in her mouth and the seam burst. She stopped reaching and she stopped growing. Even eating a donut in this peculiar place had a weird effect on her.

The strangest effect was that the bigger she got outside, the smaller she felt inside herself.

It was embarrassing though. From tall, slim, and trim, she now looked pregnant. She flipped her belt into the wastebasket. She jammed both fists under her sweater and stretched the yarn to the max to conceal her burgeoning waistline. *No more lamenting lost waistlines,* she thought. As Lenny the Lizard had said, she'd best get doing done if she was ever to get out of here.

She turned page after page, adding her own sticky crumb trail. Very likely she would have eaten the rest of the platter to keep her mind from this boring book if the grand dodo hadn't come out from behind his locked door, feathers in a flap. "Who has been eating my donuts?" he demanded, pulling his voice up from the back of his craw and blowing words and breath past his beak in an annoying whine.

"If you're referring to the donuts, I ate some."

"Any dodo can see that," he said, eyeing her ballooning waist. "That was there for the training session. Any leftovers are for me," he said, grabbing the tray and turning back to his office.

His butt had become quite fat in addition to his plump middle. It parted the pleat in his suit coat. The donuts and whatever else he'd been eating behind closed doors obviously had the same effect on him as on Alice. *Who is he to point eyes at my ballooning waist while his butt is doing the same thing?* She suppressed a giggle. *No woman dodo is ever going to follow him and say nice ass.*

He went into his office and reemerged with a foot-high stack of papers. He slapped them on Alice's desk. He moaned into his wings, holding his head feathers. "Oh, my beak and feathers. The duchess will rightsize me unless this is finished by tomorrow's session. With my luck, she'll cut off my head, and there I'll be, running around with no head, unable to see where I am going."

"What shall I do with the papers?" she asked.

"Word process them, of course. By now you should have read the book. It's what I hired you to do. I am so excited. I am developing you past your expectations."

"I had no expectations except to get out of here."

"Get these papers processed and use your head or the duchess will have your head too if you don't pull this off." He turned in a swirl of feathers and crumbs and said, "Twenty-five copies of all that in separate binders. Tomorrow you can do the in-basket. This is a wonderful challenge for you, an opportunity," he said as he caught the spin of the revolving door out.

"More like a giant headache and no aspirin in sight," Alice muttered. She suppressed a groan and reached for the rest of the donut on the napkin. The bites made her feel better. They didn't make unreasonable demands, even though her waist immediately swelled and her stomach rolled over the waistband of her skirt.

The top page of the Dodo's stack was titled "B.S. Session." *What a shocking thing to name it!* She quickly thumbed to the next page. At least B.S. was not what she had first thought.

Biz Speak Session #2010

The costmonger contabulations demand a downsteepy-sizing.[1] Downsteepysizing is not to be confused with any previous plans a.k.a. reorganization, restructuring, rightsizing, reengineering and most certainly not down-sizing. Build a new Corporateland for a better tomorrow with this totally new circumbendibas simplicity plan. It's a state-of-the-art downsteepysizing. World class. Implement with freneticized, spin-in-circles frenzy. Two gobbets exist where one should be. Bend departments into tighter circles. Leveragate[2] out surplus gobbets.[3] Reduce the head count by half and double the speed on those gobbets who remain.

---

1   Precipitous, steep descent.
2   Move, lift out the door.
3   A piece of flesh. Politically correct buzz word adopted by Gobbet Resources to encompass the wide animal/human diversity in Corporateland.

Game Plan

A surprise firedrill signals the start of the games to bring all gobbets onto the lawn.

Immediately leveragate one gobbet against the other for the first ever Downsteepysizing Games. Wondering when and who loses can lead to a paranoidization of the gobbets and an immobilized clutching of paper stacks. The best gobbet wins with this leveragated concept. The gobbet winner in each game takes home the gold, a gold foil-wrapped chocolate-covered Oreo. To bolster morale and ensure a dedicated team effort, demand an enthusiastic attitude from the winning gobbet.

Alice thought, *A gold wrapped Oreo is an exciting prize? And who can get enthused about doing twice the work?* And she couldn't understand calling them games as if this were recreation in an amusement park or a sporting event. Yet she turned the page and typed on.

All others receive involuntary quittance papers as guards escort them out the entrance gate. It's a career alternative enhancement program. It's a win-win situation. His Highness and the Duchess of Rightsizing, henceforth to be known as the Duchess of Downsteepysizing, are scheduled to sing a duet to the departed, written for this occasion.

Alice mused, *Whoever thinks this up must be so thick-headed as to think that the gobbets are so nit-witted as to believe that losing a job is a new career program Corporateland just thought up.* She swept her bangs off her forehead with a large whoosh of expelled breath and thought, *More blather, twaddle, and gabble.*

Everyone gets to play in the Games except for you, his Highness's top gobbets. Alas, you must work as Da Judges for Da Games.

His Highness magnanimously proclaims a day of play, a just-for-fun-for-all, free-for-all on the lawn, under the trees, and in the circus Big Top food tent. Sandwiches, snacks, and beverages will be available for purchase throughout the festivities. His Exaltedness grants a special boon; his subjects may come in casual attire.

That's baloney they're selling under a circus big top, Alice thought. *This is a circus all right, minus any merrymaking.* But she flipped the page and typed on.

Post-Game Activities

When the last decapitalized (note: decapitalization is not to be confused with decapitation) gobbet leaves the premises, remaining gobbets assume the work of the departed. Put the big end of the work at the small end of the day to free up daytime hours. Time-share previous daytime work with the night. This innovative plan is efficiency at its most creative and further prevents the paralyzation of profit procedure.

Alice paused in her typing and thought. *They want them to work 24/7, pull all-nighters, and do twice as much. Sounds like innovative gibberish.* But she wiggled her stiff fingers and typed on.

His Highness has authorized a mentoring program with Butter Both Sides of Their Bread Consultants. In recognition of his Highness's loneliness at the top, they promised to be a good sounding board and listener to him. They guaranteed to shave strokes off his game to slam dunk it for Corporateland in return for his Highness's expenditure of two hundred thousand dollars per month.

Alice pulled her fingers from the keys and quelled the urge to pluck the entire alphabet from the keyboard. *His Highness doesn't know what he is doing, but he's laying out a wad of cash to have someone else tell him what to do.*

The machine beeped and burped and flashed lights at her. She concluded that this was a signal she had done something wrong and set about to discover what. After many crumpled paper starts, she'd only finished two pages. The day was ending, and there was the grand dodo, his shiny black loafers with the little leather tassels jumping and soles clicking across the floor. "Well, let's see it," he said.

"I'm afraid it's not done, but if—"

"Not done. She'll have your head. She'll have my head. Oh, my beak and feathers," he said. His wing tips held each side of his head, unaware that the long feathers on top had flopped over to one side. Speckled dots of perspiration collected on the shiny molten spot.

"I was about to say," Alice said, "if you'll let me have until tomorrow morning, I think I can finish it."

"Oh, my beak and feathers. Our heads will roll," he moaned.

Crossing all of her fingers behind her back, she said, "Instead of all this moaning and groaning and talk of heads rolling, just leave me alone. I'll stay the night and finish it. You'll see. Whatever I set my mind to do, I just do it."

"Oh, my beak and feathers," he repeated. "Here, you can have the rest of my donuts; I'm not feeling well," he said, depositing the almost-empty platter with two dried, crusty circles beside her. You'll need this too," he said, holding up a rectangular blue card between two feathers. "Follow me."

He led her down the corridor. At the end was a large door that reached to the ceiling. Next to the fine wood molding set in shiny black marble walls was a square black box with a red light winking in the center. He rubbed the blue card against the red light. The door clicked and he turned the knob.

Inside was a long oval table with padded black leather chairs pulled in under oak-wood edges. Wooden cabinets with sparkling glass windows held sculpted seals of shining gold and sterling silver, some of faceted crystal and others of smooth lead crystal, still others in pewter and intricate cloisonné designs and carved ivory, all depicting the corporate seal balanced in various poses on a rock. In some, the seal's mouth greedily waited for a fish. In others, the seal was slightly cross-eyed, balancing a ball on his nose, and in still others, the seal slapped its flippers for no apparent reason.

A large picture window overlooked a small lake. Alice sucked in her breath. It was the first time she had seen daylight since falling into the paper pit. At the center of the lake was a large stone seal spouting a spray of water high into the air. A breeze blew the water into falling dollar signs that grew to bigger dollar signs upon the water. Precisely cut green grass edged the walkways, which were painted with end-to-end hundred-dollar bills traveling around the water.

Alice pointed. "What's that kelly-green alligator doing floating in the lake?"

"It's an inflatable alligator. Brilliant move by his Highness to get rid of the Canadian geese. They wandered the grounds idly eating grass, using the private drive to his royal chambers to relieve their digestive tracts of the grass clippings. His Mercedes' tires were slick with the stuff, causing an awful stink. Now they stay away since they put in the alligator," the dodo said.

Alice chuckled. Then she stared, jaw open, eyes wide. Green topiary hedges trimmed and clipped into corporate seals rose rather haughtily over the money-painted pavement. Privet hedges pruned into fifteen-foot dollar signs marched in military order around the perimeter of the grounds. At the far end, a large maze about the size of a football field was being clipped and groomed by hedge trimmers. Beyond the maze was what looked like a fence, except it was of some shiny material that reflected the sun. In the blink of an eye, the shine disappeared and was replaced by a misty smoke. "What's that shiny fence thing that just turned to smoke?" Alice asked.

"Smoke and mirrors," said the dodo.

"What is it for?"

"It's a clever illusion created by the Corporateland computer magicians intended to deceive anyone foolish enough to think there is a way out beyond the maze." His feathers stood up on end and he shuddered. "It's been rumored that a few have gone that way and have never been seen again."

Alice felt excitement rumble up through her and said, "That might be the way out, mightn't it?" She tugged at his vest like an impatient child. "Mightn't it?" she repeated.

He removed her hands from his vest and smoothed it. He ignored her and poked his flustered neck feathers back inside his shirt collar. "Come. Come. We mustn't dawdle. This is where I want you to put the books when you finish. One in front of each chair."

Alice could tell no more information was passing his beak. She thought, *There really is a way out. I just know it. Now that I know the layout of the grounds, I'll find a way to go there.*

The dodo continued, "Now mind you, this is highly confidential information. Don't breathe a word of it."

"I'll hardly breathe at all with the weight of all this work," Alice whispered under breath.

"Don't lose the card. I shall collect it in the morning. Above all, don't disturb anything in this room.

"Only *the* top executives are allowed in this room, but we are dealing with a crisis situation." *The* rolled out over his tongue like a particular appetizer he relished. "I am late for dinner."

Alice doubted, judging by his middle, that he ever missed any meal, much less dinner. He made it sound like missing dinner was the crisis, not the threat of the duchess. He left without so much as a polite thank-you or good-bye and let her find her way back down the corridor to her designated work area.

Alice worked on into the night through Inventory Shrinkage of Gobbet instructions. She giggled. She and the bird could both stand a good donut shrinking. She typed on.

New dollarized reduction plan: reduce gobbet payment mechanisms. *Except* for his Highness's top gobbets; increase their payment mechanisms and add bonuses. His Highness's payment mechanism receives a 30-percent increase, additional stock options, and a 30-percent bonus for implementing this new simplicity plan.

Not only do the remaining gobbets do twice as much work, Alice thought, *they now receive less pay. The top dudes don't know what they are doing but are pocketing a bundle of new cash while they are doing it. What sense does any of this make?* She sighed as she flexed her fingers and returned to the instructions.

Change monarchy division name from the Eastern Paper Potentate to Eastern Paper Outback. And job titles from Eastern Paper Pushers to Eastern

Paper Peddlers. And all the shapes on the organizational charts are now to be rectangles to represent miniature 8 ½ x 11 inch sheets of paper instead of squares.

Do they ever wonder, wondered Alice, *that sometimes they are not really changing anything at all?*

Alice typed on, her fingers flying as her arms ached. Her eyes burned. Her shoulders twitched. The machine hardly burped or whistled at her anymore. She and it were a single smooth hum. She zipped through a memo headed "B.S. Determinator":

In these changing times, it is important that the management team be consistent. Consistent statements. Consistent language. Carry your pocket-sized B.S. Determinator with you at all times. Use it often.

The procedure is simple: select any three words or think of any three-digit number, then select the corresponding biz-speak words. One from column A, one from column B, and one from column C. It is against copyright laws to sell these word combinations to Chinese restaurants for fortune cookies. All word combinations become the property of Corporateland. Drop these phrases into any report, letter, or memo. No one understands what you've written, but the important thing is no one will admit it.

Column A	Column B	Column C
0. fractionated	0. incremental	0. obstupefication
1. downsteepysized	1. transitional	1. jabberwocky
2. acclumsied	2. in-depth	2. tweedledumbization
3. dollarized	3. slantdicular	3. output
4. curiouser & curiouser	4. policy	4. quittance
5. circumbendibas	5. in-depth	5. financialization
6. decruitmetized	6. ambiguous	6. contabulation
7. financialized	7. bumptuous	7. input
8. moronological	8. management	8. functionality
9. bunkfied	9. synergistical	9. costmongers

Everything gets curiouser and curiouser, Alice thought, flexing her numb fingers. *Sounds like bumptuous moronological jabberwocky*. She yawned, borrowing from columns A, B, and C. Sometimes intelligence creates a lot of confusion. She'd learned about speaking her mind. She wouldn't this time. She'd again be lectured about education and degrees and not knowing what she thought she knew. She'd bide her time and wait for the crack in a door somewhere to get out of here. She stretched and yawned again. Her fingers were clumps. Her mind felt like thick tree stumps as she turned to the last page.

At last Alice placed the finished booklets at each place around the table just as a blood-red sun was inching its way up over the lake out the picture window. She patted the control card in her pocket to assure herself she had not lost it. She closed the door and walked back to her desk, curled one arm around her head on her desk, and pressed her cheek against a mound of papers.

As she drifted toward the luxury of sleep, a whisper brushed her ear. "Psst." She ignored it and batted at it as if flicking away gnats. *This is just that time between sleep and dreams*, she thought and yawned. Or maybe it was the dodo with another request. He could wait.

"Psst," persisted the voice in her ear, but she was too tired to look up to see who or where it was coming from. The voice said, "The computer wizards wrote an exception in the smoke and mirrors program. It's a closely guarded secret. When you get to the mirror, you *can* walk through. You just have to believe you can."

Alice mumbled, "Then why doesn't everyone leave?"

The disembodied voice continued, "They believe what the computer wizards told them. No one can get through. Remember, all you have to do is believe you can. It's very simple, but that doesn't mean that simplicity doesn't have its difficulty."

"Yes, whatever," Alice murmured and fell into a deep sleep. It seemed only moments after that the sharp quill of a feather was poking her. "I have good news and bad news," the grand dodo said.

Alice shook her head to clear away sleep and the strange dream with the whispering voice.

"Could it wait?" Alice tipped her head and looked up. She blinked eyes that itched and burned. She peeled off a sheet of paper stuck to her cheek and put her head back on the desk.

"It can't wait. The duchess was very pleased with this session I put on this morning. Very pleased she was. Probably means a promotion for me."

"I'm very happy for you." Alice yawned again. "Now what's the bad news?"

"Your job grade has been reduced two levels, profit procedure and all," he said.

Her head snapped up. She was fully awake now with a growing sense of dread. She swallowed back an angry retort and nearly gave him a piece of what was left of her mind. "That means I'm lower than working in the paper pit. What good is hard work, if it hardly gets me anywhere?"

"It gets you here," he said, thrusting several pages in a manila file at her. "Get approvals. I need fifty-seven approvals before the end of this day. Orders from the duchess." And he flapped off without his wings lifting him from the ground.

Today Alice felt the most depressed since falling down the paper tunnel. She sat in front of the screen, her neck stiff, her shoulders shooting sharp pains, her legs numb from sitting, her eyes puffy, and her head dizzy from lack of sleep and staring at the screen. All the words in the manila file blurred together. She left it lying on the desk. *Maybe*, she thought, *if I take a walk down the corridor, I'll feel better.*

She thought she was going the same way as before, but she knew she wasn't when she found herself in a very long corridor. Everywhere she went in this place there were halls and walls and corridors filled with doors. All of them opened in, but none ever got her out. It was like a giant maze and no solution to the puzzle. Doors in this corridor cut into the gray walls. A gray tweed carpet ran like a path to the end, which was so far in the distance it was a blur. Or maybe that was her dizzy head; she couldn't tell. Each door was closed. Firmly shut. Except one with voices drifting into the hall. She walked toward the voices.

A curious thing began to happen. Her stomach started shrinking. The farther away from the training track she got, the smaller it got. She forgot her dizzy head as she palmed her stomach to check the progress with each step. She knew she really ought to keep going past the door with the voices or go back. She stopped, and so did her new reducing plan, as she peered in the door, which was half ajar. She got very excited. There was a man, a human, inside. Maybe he'd show her the way out as one human to another.

Madsen Hatter and Adorable Mouse

This was the first human she had encountered in Corporateland. Her excitement was quickly dispelled. A strange man wearing six hats stacked one atop the other was seated next to a dormouse with long blonde hair at a conference table. He appeared to be suffering from a bad case of a stress disorder. His eyes glittered but were not alert and watchful—more like they would go spinning in the sockets at any moment. He sat complacently next to the dormouse, who blinked her blue eyes at him rather adoringly and seemingly had no concern over his quite mad and frenzied look. She slid her long finger nails in, under, and around the silk scarf flowing from her breast pocket as if to draw attention to the fact that they were the exact shade as the fire-red flecks in the gold scarf. A BlackBerry sat idle in front of each of them. A blue manila file in front of the mouse perfectly matched her royal-blue suit and royal-blue shoes.

"Did you bring the green file, Adorable Mouse?" asked the man with the hats.

"No, Mad. I couldn't today. It did not properly match my outfit," she said.

"Dora, how many times have I told you? Never ever call me Mad. You can call me Madsen. You can call me Hatter. You can call me Hat. But never ever call me Mad." He spit the words through clenched teeth as his eyes started to twirl in their sockets.

Dipping her head, her paws shaking, Dora said, "I'm sorry, Madsen."

"Don't let it happen again. Since you don't have the green file, we will address that at our next meeting."

"I shall have to buy a new outfit," she said. "I have nothing to go with green."

"Well, yes, whatever. I move we start."

"You start," she said.

"No, you start," he said.

They batted those words back and forth at each other while Alice swiveled her head back and forth like she was a spectator at a tennis match. When neither of them started anything, Alice could contain herself no longer. "Start what?" she asked.

"The staff meeting, of course," they both replied.

Her eyes traveled the large round table. All the chairs were empty except for theirs. "But you have no staff," she said.

Madsen Hatter pulled up his slumped shoulders and puffed his chest. "We are managers who have been appointed to manage without them."

"Yes," the adorable mouse said, flouncing her gold scarf with her long red nails, "we manage without them."

"Did you ever have a staff?" Alice asked.

"Oh yes, but the duchess found it necessary in this recent company-wide rightsizing to eliminate all overhead. She ran around for days shouting, 'off with their heads.'"

"That's cruel and absurd," Alice said.

"That's necessary to profit procedure, and besides, the duchess can be terribly savage if we don't do what she wants," Madsen Hatter replied, rolling his glassy eyes to the ceiling.

"Yes, profit procedure and terribly savage," Adorable Mouse echoed, buffing her nails on her jacket.

"Who does the work the staff did?" At Alice's question,

a wrapped bundle of pink papers whistled by her ear. She jumped as the missile landed with a thwack, smack in the middle of the table.

"Did you notice, Dora, the messenger service is getting more accurate every day?" Madsen Hatter asked. Then he addressed Alice. "Sometimes they couldn't even hit the table. A lot of messages got lost that way." He slid the stack of messages toward the dormouse, who slid them back. "Oh, by and by we'll be hiring new people," he said to no one in particular. They continued this sliding back and forth much as they had the "Start. No, you start" conversation.

"That's absurd," Alice said. "Why did you get rid of staff if you're only going to hire more?"

"Executive decisions," Madsen spouted. "We are downsizing the previous upsizing to reengineer to the right size at a later date."

"Yes, executive decisions," the dormouse repeated.

"Why weren't you part of the duchess's overhead cuts? Though I wouldn't want to wish that on anyone, I just can't see the reasoning for keeping managers with no staff."

"We are far too important. We are the right size. The others weren't. Strategic positions, that's what we have. They gave us gold balloons to keep us here," Madsen said.

"Balloons are nice and all, and, Adorable Mouse, I can see a gold one would be lovely with your outfit today, but how is that an incentive to keep you here?"

"The gold balloons are inflated payment mechanisms. I have more money to buy more clothes. We stay in this period of the downsizing to aid in the later upsizing. By and by everyone will all be the right size."

As they talked, Madsen arranged and rearranged the stack of messages. Carefully, with the tip of his tongue protruding just beyond his teeth, he shuffled the stack like a deck of cards, dealt them to the table top, and then scooped them up and aligned them meticulously beside each other like he was playing a game of solitaire judged on neatness. He rebunched them and started all over again.

"Why do you keep shuffling the messages?"

"As a hedge against the duchess's headhunters. You never know when more heads will be cut. I'm always prepared. That's why I wear so many hats. When they come, they will see I'm a very organized man and very good at managing my papers and can wear different hats." Whereupon he shuffled his hats on the table and tried each one on in turn. Then he stacked them one on top of another and put them back on his head.

"But, but," she sputtered, "You're just moving the papers around and trying on hats and accomplishing nothing."

His eyes got fuzzy and out of focus then, like they would go twirling at any moment. "You've been disruptive long enough; we must get back to our meeting," he answered. Turning to the dormouse, he asked, "What business do you have to discuss?"

"Yes, business to discuss," she repeated. "I move we get new chairs for our new staff. Blue, I think, to match my blue eyes." She fanned her long red nails near her eyes.

"Agreed," he said, "and let's move the wall to make the room bigger for our new staff. Have you noticed," he continued, "that staff morale is low?"

"How absurd," Alice interjected. "You have no staff."

Madsen Hatter stared at Alice, and his eyes became narrow, off-center little beads twirling out of focus. "I don't recall inviting you to have a turn."

"No, wait," the dormouse offered. "Let's let her be our staff."

"What a great idea. You can be our staff until we get a staff."

"Don't I have a choice whether I want to be included?"

"Of course not. The choices are all ours," they said together.

Madsen added, "I've needed my rental tuxedo returned, my dry cleaning picked up, and my briefcase taken to the repair shop. None of that's been done since I had my staff cut. We also need new batteries for our Blackberrys, and then we can cancel the messenger service." He pointed to the two Blackberrys laying idle on the table.

"Oh yes, and I would like you to shop for greeting cards while you are out doing those things," Dora Mouse said, checking some notes on a paper in front of her. "One birthday card, one wedding, and seven sympathy cards to the staff that isn't here anymore, plus a potted geranium for Mummy for Mother's Day and an appointment to get her toenails clipped. She hasn't had an appointment in ages. Mummy's toenails are getting ever so long."

Alice slumped in her chair. This was no more than shades of the same stuff she'd done for the prince. "Why can't you do these things yourselves? Er ... ah ... um ... since you don't seem to have anything else to do," Alice asked, her voice trailing off as Madsen Hatter aimed his twirling eyes at her.

Madsen cleared his throat. "The mental floggings will continue," he declared and aimed both eyes, which suddenly gained focus, right on Alice, "until staff moral improves."

"Yes, continue the mental floggings until staff morale improves," the dormouse echoed. Alice jumped out of her chair and ran as fast as she possibly could out the door. She sped quietly across the gray carpet toward the blur that was the end of the hall. Their feet were close on her heels.

Just when her breath was about to burst in her chest, the hall ended. In front of her was a tall narrow door and beside it another black box and winking red light. The control card! She hadn't returned it to the dodo. She pulled it from her pocket and pressed it to the red eye. The lock clicked. The door swung open. Alice ran through. It quickly slammed shut against Alice's back. On the other side, she heard Madsen Hatter and Adorable Mouse panting and puffing.

Madsen said, "We can't get in. We don't have our cards. I move we adjourn the meeting."

"Adjourn the meeting," Dora repeated. "Shall we have lunch?"

The Human Resource Cat

That was a narrow escape, Alice thought, letting the puffing and panting quiet in her chest. As she rested her back against the wall, she noticed a sign down the hall on the opposite side. She walked slowly toward it. In large black letters against shiny brass, it read Human Resources. Her heart thumped with excitement. At last, a place that handled human matters! And with the resources to help her.

She timidly knocked on the door next to the sign. "Yes. Yes. Come in. Come in," a gravelly voice said. She took a few halting, tentative steps into a large room looking out over a courtyard. Centered in the window frame was a bronze statue of a seal rising as high as the first-story window. Its head was back, its back was arched, and one flipper raised to the sky held a half circle of letters spelling out the words Founding Father Seal. Flowers puddled in reverential bundles around the base.

An enormous navy-blue cat with white whiskers sat grinning behind a large mahogany desk. A brushed brass plate at the center of his desk read HR Cat. A navy-blue and white ring-striped tail waved mesmerizingly behind him. When he pulled back his lips to smile, he exposed yellow teeth as big as piano keys from one ear to the other and from his nose to his chin. Just briefly, Alice wondered what a cat was doing handling human matters, but only for an instant. If it didn't seem likely in this strange and confusing place, it was sure to be right, no matter how wrong it seemed.

A painting of a grinning lion hung behind the cat's head. One large paw was plopped across the tail of a mouse whose feet ran in place, creating two tiny puffs of dust. The human resources cat sat behind his desk clipping his long claws with a nail clipper. As he sat clipping and grinning, his body faded in and out, except for the smile, which always stayed in the same place. He wore no clothing except starched white shirt cuffs above each paw. He shot them forward. A red stone set in gold winked in each cuff as he folded his paws on the leather blotter.

His grin looks good natured enough, Alice thought. Still, he had very long nails and a great many teeth, so she felt he ought to be treated with respect.

"HR Cat at your service. What can I do for you? Speak up now," he demanded, buffing a paw across his large teeth.

This was not the least bit encouraging, so Alice began gingerly. "I hardly know who I am at present. At least I knew before I fell down the paper tunnel, or at least I thought I did. I was just Alice then, and only late, but I didn't know for what, and that didn't seem nearly enough."

"In this time of political correctness, we want to be fair to all. While I've had more experience with matters of animal orientation, I do have a few minutes to review a human matter," the cat said sternly, drumming his clipped claws on the desk blotter.

"If you deal in animal matters, how can you know what it is like to be human?"

"I pretend like I know what I'm talking about. Come, come. You are wasting my time. Explain yourself."

Alice cleared her throat, straightened her shoulders, and in her most polite voice said, "Mr. HR Cat, I prefer someone who knows human matters and has more time." She moved toward the door.

He grinned a self-satisfied grin and said, "There is no one else."

Alice stopped before turning the doorknob. "If I explain myself, then will you show me the way out?"

"You are wasting my time. I'm leaving." And with that his body and head faded, leaving only the toothed ear-to-ear grin suspended above his chair.

"Now you stop that, Mr. HR Cat. Come back here."

"Very well, I'll give you one more chance to explain yourself," he said as one paw slowly materialized over his desk blotter and landed with a loud thump. The rest of his body snapped into view. Alice jumped at the suddenness. A claw from his other paw tapped one of his large teeth, and his tail waved behind his chair like he was stalking a mouse. "Well, I'm waiting," he said.

Alice began hurriedly. "I can't explain myself. Or at least when I do I'm told not to use my head, that I was not hired to think. Then when I ask questions, I'm told to use my head and think. And all I would really like to do is get out of here, but everyone tells me a different job is the way out, and I do the jobs and never get any further. My job has now been reduced two grades lower than when I was working for the white rabbit who had a degree in management, but by degrees I could see I knew how to manage better than he. Bunnifer Rarebit, his personal assistant, thinks her most pressing duty is polishing her nails, talking to her mother, online shopping, and taking breaks, while I was told to work harder and faster and got no breaks. Then I agreed to work for the dodo bird. Can you imagine how queer it is to work for an extinct bird? He said he would teach me, and then I taught myself and he trained others in riddles. And Madsen Hatter, who seems quite mad in a frenzied sort of way …"

The Cat put up a hand-stopping paw, "Frenzied? Mad? What's so unusual about that? We're all frenzied and quite mad around here, you know. That's why I'm sometimes here and sometimes not." As if to demonstrate, his body again faded except for his wide smile showing lots of sharp teeth.

Alice's lower lip trembled, but she asked, "What do you mean that everyone is frenzied and quite mad?"

His sharp eyes looked her up and down and said, "Corporateland, as any ninny knows, is built on frenzy and madness. How else could we do what we do if we weren't in a constant frenzy and slightly mad? When I don't want to deal with something, I disappear." As if to demonstrate, he disappeared.

Alice continued on, not about to let a fading body take away the opportunity to finish telling her experiences in this place to someone. "Well, Madsen Hatter and Dora Mouse want me to be their staff just to have a staff to give mental floggings to, and all I would really like to do is leave. Then the dodo said my job with him was reduced two grades lower than the paper pit. Now I am lower than when I started. I have no hope of ever finishing any of these jobs or getting out of here," she finished, quite out of breath.

"Well, well. No need to swallow a fur ball about this. That is what I am here for," he said, snapping back into view as he slid a metal file back and forth across his clipped nails. "I shall look at the records." He peered closely at a computer screen and made clearing noises in his throat with hums and hos and such.

Alice kept sternly telling herself not to cry or get too hopeful, as she had been disappointed all the other times before. She was used to giving herself very good advice but seldom followed it.

"Hmm, you worked for U Nick Rabbit, I see. One of the finest mismanagers to ever come from Old Misalliance University."

Alice's head jerked and her eyes popped wider. "You do understand. He is a mismanager," she said excitedly.

"Yes, one of our finest, as I said. He's studying nights now for a combined degree in Misinterpretation, Misinformation, and Misconduct."

Alice responded dryly, all excitement sucked from her voice, "He applies it every opportunity he gets during the day. He and Lenny the Lizard said and did the most sexually inappropriate and embarrassing things."

"Yes, they do have that reputation. That's why I

assigned them to the paper pit and the paper stacks, respectively." Pointing a sharp nail at Alice, HR continued. "And we had experienced no further problems with them until *you* arrived."

"Just because they are out of your sight doesn't mean their behavior went away," Alice mumbled.

"Speak up. What were you mumbling?"

"Never mind," Alice said. It was just another hopeless case of their behavior somehow being her fault.

"Well, let's continue. I see that most recently you were with the dodo, a great pathetic listener and one of our great verbal communicators," he said, peering at the screen.

"If you mean he talks a lot and rarely listens, I definitely agree."

"For an underling, you do understand good verbal communication quite well. Part of the problem may be that you may not be suited to Corporateland. Let's examine your records."

She nodded, swallowed, and held on tight, one hand gripping the other. He swiveled back to the computer screen and dipped his head so close to it that his whiskers crackled against the screen. Finally he raised his head. "It's all here. Very clearly in your records. From your last Dog Nuqx Review."

"My Dog Nuts Review?" she gasped. Then she composed herself. Perhaps this was like the B.S. Session, not at all what she first thought. She cleared her throat. "Could I please see this review?"

"Well, yes, of course. If you must see it again. You probably just forgot when the dodo gave it to you," he said impatiently. He tapped a paw on the blotter while it printed. "One never forgets. It's a time-honored tradition. Dates back to the days when the founding father seal expanded. Added more horse-drawn paper carts and an HR department. They were the innovators of the Dog Nuqx Review. Your forgetfulness is a certain sign of problems."

"I assure you. I've not had a review. I've been so busy paper processing and word processing there has been no chance."

He slid the paper to her triumphantly. "It's all here."

Corporateland

DOG NUQX REVIEW

For   Alice Wenderland

Date   Out of Date   Rating **DEGrading** (New Category)

To prevent merit mongering, performance reviews are not tied to performance. This is not a grading system like in school. We cleverly disguised the letters in a non-sequential, non-specific order so as not to tie achievement or awards to salaries. Rating determines the salary, but we shrewdly establish separate dates for each to camouflage the connection to prevent salary mongering.

D   Distinguished. Awarded posthumously or after retirement when it doesn't matter. Dangle this like a carrot as an incentive that will maybe, possibly, but never quite be awarded "the next time." There never is a next time. It's always waiting to happen, like tomorrow. When you think tomorrow has arrived, it's really today.

O   Outstanding. Rarely given for same reasons as above. Just when they have it, snatch it from them and say, "Work harder next time." Sometimes awarded to butt-buster salesmen when they make moves to bust their butts someplace else.

G   Good. Fair to middling mediocrity. Again, rarely given. Many attain it, but we can't lose our incentive plan. What would they work for next time?

N   Performance good. *Not!* Kick new employees in the teeth with this. Guaranteed to jump-start their careers and up production 100 percent. Offer sympathy and another chance.

U   Unsatisfactory. Unsatisfying. Much like the N rating. Use when your department needs revitalizing and you want to bleed new blood.

QX   Quittanced by head chopping.

DEGrading New category added to cover the recent upgrading that needed downgrading.

"The payment mechanism committee has decided that your recent upgrading needed downgrading because it does not run parallel to profit procedure. After all, you just pushed paper around."

"Oh, so did Madsen Hatter and Lenny the Lizard," she retorted. Her insides began sizzling, but then she bit her lips and tried to think calmly. "It seems you're saying that for the company to make money, my salary has to be reduced."

"No, no, my dear girl. No salary reduction. You will still receive two cents an hour, which, I might add, is the highest salary we give in the DEGrading category. Only your grade level has been reduced."

"This is just a bunch of puffed up double-talk," Alice said hotly, "I get my job grade reduced so I won't get further raises and I continue to do more work than ever before and the company continues to get ahead and Madsen Hatter and Dora Mouse get raises to manage no staff."

"Precisely. For a rather common-looking girl, you do understand quite precisely. Now it is precisely time for another appointment, so if you would be so kind as to leave," he said as his body dissolved leaving only his starched cuff pointing at the door.

"I do want to leave, and you were my last hope, but you don't have any better answers than the others." Then her eyes, despite her better sense, began spilling large saucer-sized tear drops onto his desk.

"Here. Here. You'll get my leather blotter wet," HR said, materializing. He threw a box of paper tissues in her lap. "The problem, as I see it, is you are trying to be reasonable and logical. Do not try to be reasonable or logical, or you could get lost in the system for days."

"That's it! That's it! I have been lost in the system," she said, jumping up with a handful of crumpled tissues clutched in her fist, glad to hold on to any understanding. HR Cat drummed his clipped nails on the blotter in hard staccato taps while she blew her nose rather loudly into one of the tissues. "Could you please tell me just one thing? Then I'll go."

He let all of his nails fall on the blotter in one hard clump and held them that way, poised for more impatient drumming.

"Could you please tell me which is the way out of here?" she asked, shredding the soggy tissues.

"That depends on where you want to go."

"It doesn't really matter, as long as it's somewhere out of here."

"There you go; it doesn't matter. Just keep walking; you're sure to get there," he said, fading. His toothy smile, minus a head, and his long pin-striped tail, minus a body, floated past Alice out of the room.

The Corporate Seal Games

Now she really was the most depressed since landing in this place but had no time to give in to the feeling. She had no sooner left HR Cat's office than she heard screaming from behind another closed door down the hall. Animals and birds of every shape, size, and description gathered along the corridor and looked grave and serious.

The group in the hall rushed to the second-floor windows overlooking the lake and lawn. Alice mashed her nose to the glass with the rest of the creatures. Below them the lawn was filled with even more corporate seals perched on stones. A sky box above held his Highness. His hollow graphic image was front and center, but he looked grim and about to chew a hoof.

"It's the Corporate Seal Games that are about to begin," a turkey said, his red wattle bobbing up and down on his throat. "We've been hearing rumblings about them for weeks. The Bisneyworld Crowned Executive Omnipotent is being forced to play in the Seal Games to prevent a hostile takeover by Corporateland. The duchess of rightsizing is playing for his Highness in the games in recognition for her efficiency in cutting heads. He lowered his voice to a squawking whisper. "And who is more hostile than the duchess? She better win all the corporate seals from Bisneyworld, or his Highness will have her head."

Alice felt very uneasy. She had no dispute with the duchess, but in this place they were dreadfully fond of beheading overhead; it was a wonder anyone was left. She wondered what was to become of her.

In thinking about it afterward, she never could remember exactly how it happened. One minute she was just standing next to the turkey, and the next minute a screaming blur of red ran out the door and stopped immediately in front of Alice. The blur evolved into a red-faced bull-doggish creature. Alice couldn't decide if it was an animal or human. It had two shining red beacons fore and aft. It had pressed its short rotund ball of a body into knee-hugging red spandex pants and a silky red top.

"Well," the red apparition haughtily asked, "Who is this strange creature, and what is your business?"

With a quaking voice, Alice said, "No, you misunderstand. I just want to leave, if someone will show me the way out. It's all because I followed the white rabbit."

The next moment, the red creature had grabbed Alice's hand, and it seemed they were flying through space, but nothing moved except its feet. "Your feet are spinning just like in the dodo's training session."

"Of course. That's Basic Management 101," the creature grandly intoned. "I have to go this fast just to stay in the same place."

Alice held on and soon was panting in place. "That's all that happens here. Lots of running and then your head gets chopped if you don't run fast enough. No one says a positive word to anyone."

"Not my job," the creature said. "I am the head chopper."

Alice gulped. "*You* are the duchess?"

Her beady little eyes bored into Alice. She licked her fat lips. "Of course. Who else would I be? You may kiss my ring," she said and extended her hand.

Alice broke out in a cold sweat and felt weak in the knees. However, she achieved a contorted curtsey while running in place and then tipped her head over the ruby-red ring, which bore an etched likeness of the duchess replete with chubby cheeks. Before she could kiss the ring, the duchess quickly extracted her hand.

"Well, speak up and be quick about it," the duchess said.

Alice stumbled over her words. "Well, we had not met, and I've only heard of you by reputation." She hurried on quickly, "Your head-chopping ability is probably state-of-the-art, and I can see you are an extremely fast runner."

The corner of one of the duchess's fat lips started to turn up in the suggestion of a smile as if she was maybe possibly just the teeny tiniest bit pleased.

Alice felt a glimmer of hope that the fat redhead next to her might be capable of reason. "See, I can tell you were pleased with a compliment. What if you started complimenting workers and production increased? Then I'll bet employees would no longer be afraid of you."

The duchess quickly returned the lip to its straight hard line, pulled herself up, and roared, "Afraid? Who's afraid? The recent employee survey gave me the highest rating ever, and employee surveys never lie. Everyone knows they can answer honestly. They honestly like me."

"Right," Alice muttered sarcastically between pants.

"It's clear that you are not suited to Corporateland. Guards! Guards! Off with her head! She clearly can't think, and she can't run fast enough."

With that, Alice collapsed on the ground, unable to run anymore. She rubbed the leather instep of each boot to soothe her aching arches. "No, I just want to leave, and everyone keeps telling me a different way is the way out, and no one makes any sense," she said.

"All the ways are mine," the duchess said with a toss of her red head, "by appointment of his Highness. *I* don't have to make sense," the duchess yelled. "I am the vice president of downsizing, rightsizing, and the new downsteepysizing program. *And*"—she paused and drew herself up as tall as she could and peered along her inclined nose at Alice—"I am playing in the Corporate Seal Games to win all the Bisneyworld corporate seals for his Highness of Corporateland. Yay team. I'll deal with you later."

The duchess grabbed a slippery seal from a guard. She stood, one arm akimbo, with the seal hammer locked under one arm. It began barking loudly and slapping its flippers while she got redder by degrees. At first Alice though the duchess was holding her breath. If she was, it served to inflate her; she grew larger, redder, and more imposing until she stood before them—an inflated, oppressive behemoth of her former self.

Alice leaped back and knocked over the turkey. She just missed stamping her foot on his wrinkled red neck and tripped in a heap among his feathers. She lay there all ruffled, teeth chattering with terror, until she saw that the duchess was running as fast as her legs could maneuver down the hall. The duchess's backside rose and fell in cadence with the seal's tail section whacking her butt on the rise and fall. Its front flippers flapped and slapped, and it barked with a wide, whiskered mouth. Alice could smell his fishy breath as they passed. Her alarm turned to a fit of giggles. She smashed her hand over her mouth to hide the smile and mask the giggles. Alice thought, *How bizarre that his Highness put this creature, who'd probably dipped into the same donut tray as she and the dodo, in charge of a staff reduction plan.* The duchess could do with a whole body reduction plan herself.

The duchess stomped onto the lawn. Her heavily endowed bust jiggled and jumped while her aft section wiggled and woggled with the seal's tail section still rhythmically whacking her backside. The whole scene was like a red cape at a bull fight, which was fitting, because the Bisneyworld CEO emerged from the end of the playing field pawing the turf and bellowing and snorting and shaking his hairy head like the bull he was. His white silk boxing shorts fell to a point below his knees. A Fruit of the Loom buckle was emblazoned at his waist, while red suspenders snapped over his massive chest and torso. Without so much as a starting pistol, a referee's whistle, or "The Star Spangled Banner," he came charging straight for the duchess with his own corporate seal balancing a ball on his nose.

The duchess wielded her seal like a bat and walloped the ball off the nose of the CEO's seal. The duchess squinted against the sky and tried to track the high fly ball. "Advantage me. Advantage me," she yelled, her chubby knees pumping up and down.

"Advantage me," he yelled back and threw a net over her seal's head and dragged it straight down the middle to his side of the field.

She picked another seal from a rock and shouted in a voice like thunder, "You stole my seal. I shall not permit it!" and charged the CEO. The ball fell off her seal's nose. Dipping her seal at a slight downward angle, she used it as a hockey stick and dribbled the ball down centerfield. With a flick of his head, the CEO signaled his fair-haired function executive, who sneaked up behind the duchess and popped her seal from the crook in her arm with a shove of his own seal's flipper. The duchess snatched up two new seals, one in each arm.

The Bisneyworld CEO stepped forward till the

Bisneyworld corporate seal was nose-to-nose with one of the Corporateland seals. The duchess did a quick step backward, crouched, and with a fast up-thrust into Fair-Haired's midsection dropped him to his backside. She plunked one seal on his face and pinned him in the mud. She then took a deep breath and lunged forward with the other seal, its flippers raised menacingly at the CEO's face. It let loose two sharp wet slaps, one to each of his cheeks, and tweaked his nose with its mouth. He retreated a short distance. Determined to press her advantage, the duchess went for his seal and plucked out its whiskers in quick, vigorous plucks.

The Bisneyworld CEO looked like he was suffering a bad case of indigestion, hemorrhoids, *and* ulcers. The duchess was panting. Recharging herself, Alice supposed. The panting was very shortly shattered by a piercing wail coming straight from her mouth. She opened it so wide that Alice could see the back of her throat and her uvula all red and bulbous like the tip of a large thermometer. "I want them *all*. *All* of the seals, I tell you." And she stamped her foot much like Alice's niece did when she didn't get the sweets she wanted.

The wailing masked the CEO's next attack. He took his left shoe off and inserted the toe right up to the laces in the duchess's gaping mouth. "Eat shoe leather you will," he was heard to curse under his breath.

The duchess grew even redder in the face and began waving her arms at the guards, pointing to the offending shoe. Even her eyes were red, on a scorch so intense that all the guards hung back immobilized. The duchess's knees crumpled. She flopped on the ground and rolled to her back. Finally an old toad, the old guard from the paper tunnel, splatted his feet across the concrete and planted a splayed foot in the middle of her stomach while he yanked with both upper arms to remove the impacted shoe. "The seals are ours," she managed to croak through clenched teeth as if to prevent another impaction.

"I assume you are much too weak to rule," the CEO said.

"You," the duchess began, pulling herself up grandly from the concrete. "You are a pain in the assumption." She began making windmill motions with both arms and shouted in a gravelly voice, "Get to your places." Ten animals of various species and ranks came running from all directions to the duchess's side of the field. At the same time the Bisneyworld CEO signaled his entourage. Everyone began grabbing seals.

It was shambles. It was chaos. The seals yelped "yurk, yuk," and "yeak, yeak," punctuated at intervals with the slippery bashing.

The chief difficulty was for everyone to figure out how to handle their seals. They would succeed in getting the body tucked under their arms with the flippers hanging out the front and the tail section out the back; but just when they had succeeded in getting the head straight to strike a blow, the seal would twist itself around and look up into the handler's face with a puzzled expression as if to say "Why?"

Some, unable to handle the slippery bodies, dropped their seals. They helplessly crawled on their bellies toward the pond, only to be scooped up by whoever was near. Some made it to the water and swam to the stone seal in the center. Some hung onto the inflated kelly-green alligator. This set off quarreling and arguing over the remaining seals and pulling and tugging of the seal bodies, one player at the head and the other at the tail, till Alice thought sure they would split in two.

The crashing and smashing and jarring and jerking caused such a ruckus that Alice observed books and binders jumping off shelves from an open doorway across the hall. The group in the hall scattered for whatever cover was near. Dora Mouse jumped into the arms of HR Cat, ignoring his very sharp teeth and sharp claws. HR did one of his fade-outs and Dora looked like she was suspended in air courtesy of her long flowing silk scarf. No one noticed, especially Madsen Hatter, who curled under a nearby desk and rolled a chair in after him, his glassy eyes twirling, peering out from under the legs.

The dodo whined, "My head and feathers. Oh, my head and feathers." In lieu of a donut, he stuck his thumb feather in his beak and made slurping noises that would never have been acceptable if one was dining. The thumb feather became matted and raggedy.

The white rabbit hopped his hind legs behind a stack of binders, wringing the front ones, squeaking, "Oh, worry and bother. Oh, worry and bother."

The whacking and smacking and bashing and crashing built to such a crescendo that the very foundation on which the building stood began rocking and swaying. The intensity was so great that everyone abandoned their places of cover inside, and all sorts of birds and beasts began pouring outside onto the lawn and taking up positions behind the bushes and hedges near the playing field. Alice crawled under a hedge near the front. The sidelines seemed paralyzed except for selective whispering about their fate. Another group gathered behind the potted plants near the cafeteria windows despite the quaking and shaking.

"What do you think of the games?" a voice asked.

Alice looked up into a piano-keyed grin suspended in the air above the hedge. An ear, then two eyes, and then his whole head materialized around the grin. Dora jumped down and scurried away. "Well, what do you think of the games?" he asked.

"I don't think they play fairly," Alice said, "and they quarrel so dreadfully they can't hear themselves speak, and they don't have any rules in particular. It's just a bunch of impolite animals running around seeing who can grab the most seals. And if the duchess doesn't get her way, she stamps her foot and yells quite loudly."

"I know," he said, fading to a grin.

Alice stamped her foot. "Why do you keep disappearing like that?"

"One never knows when the duchess," he said, coming into focus, "may decide to replace me, but she can't remove a head from a body if there isn't one." And he faded completely away once more.

Back on the field, the CEO began shouting, "You are trying to steal my seals. I shall not permit it. Counsel. Counsel. Legal Counsel. Extract me from the duchess's machinations."

All the CEO's legal eagles, powdered wigs askew, flew in with their legal colors flying. "We pronounce she can legally do this. You are quite null and void. She has more seals than you do and the fish to feed them. You could become your own debt instrument, but pound for pound, Corporateland's got the fish to buy out and feed your seals."

Then the most curious thing happened. Everyone abandoned their seals, who let a few weak "yurk, yurks" and flopped on the concrete walk, too tired to go to the water. They huddled together, and soon the whole mass of seals was rhythmically snoring long, loud, snurking snores.

All of Corporateland's legal eagles and all of Bisneyworld's legal eagles joined wings, dancing in a circle around his Highness and the CEO. They sang:

It's a beautiful soup, so rich and green.
A beautiful soup. So rich and green.
We shall all be richer than we've ever dreamed.
We shall all be richer than we've ever dreamed.

In an incentivized contabulation, Bisneyworld's CEO accepted a seat on his Highness's team. His fair-haired consort was dazed after his collision with the duchess, but he quickly switched balls and successfully changed into Corporateland colors. His Highness from Corporateland and the Bisneyworld CEO could be seen clutching stock options and lump-sum cash bonuses dancing on the field hoof-to-hoof while the legal eagles sang:

It's a beautiful soup, so rich and green.
A beautiful soup. So rich and green.
We shall all be richer than we've ever dreamed.
We shall all be richer than we've ever dreamed.

Corporateland and Bisneyworld issued a joint accuracy and simplicity statement:

> In this transitional-time phase, a circumbendibas moronological simplicity plan is being put in place with freneticized, run-in-circles frenzy. Gobbets are our most important asset. But where there are two jobs, there will now be one. This requires that departing gobbets move their assets and slam dunk them elsewhere. All remaining gobbets will participate in the new state-of-the-art, world-class Downsteepysizing Games.

At this point, the joint statement was interrupted by a loudspeaker booming "Hear ye. Hear ye. Through a stroke of sheer genius, the duchess has created a new sporting event as an introduction to the Downsteepysizing Games. All Corporateland gobbets are to run an amazing maze race through the newly completed corporate maze.

"The maze race is an ethnic cleansing of whole departments as a quick head-cutting method to free up more cash to pay for the corporate seals we acquired in the Bisneyworld take over. Everyone not eliminated in the maze race is then eligible for the previously announced Downsteepysizing Games pitting Corporateland gobbets against Bisneyworld gobbets, where further frenzied head-chopping will ensue.

"In a special boon and because the duchess is in a sporting mood after her win, she condescendingly grants that that human Alice person can run with the rest of the animals in the amazing maze race. She is being given one last chance to prove she belongs in Corporateland."

Alice had never been good at games, and here she was going to have to play another one. Her heart plummeted, and her mind jumped from thought to thought. She'd seen that maze from the conference-room window when she was with the dodo bird. It ran in a confusing rectangle that spread over an area the size of a football field, and the walls were at least nine feet high, and the interior path had so many stops and starts and roadblocks and dead ends as to suggest there was never a way out. The hedge seemed thick and impassable without tools to cut through. She suddenly remembered the voice in her dream. If it was true, there was an outside hope that the smoke-and-mirrors fence on the other side was maybe, just maybe, a way out. If she could just make it through the maze ...

"Hedge trimmers, to your places," the duchess shouted.

Gardeners with hedge clippers clutched menacingly to their chests appeared every five feet at the top of the hedges. The head hedge trimmer loudly announced, "Don't hedge your bets on anything anymore. Do not collect gold when you pass go. There is no get-out-of-jail-free card. No gold watch for thirty years of devoted service. No one is allowed to leave before his time. Only leave at the appropriate dead-end sign."

Alice asked timidly, "How will we know what that is?"

"A flashing red neon finger will point at you, and a voice from a boom box in central headquarters will say, 'This means you.'"

Her lip trembling, Alice asked, "You mean without a thank-you or a kind word to wish you well on your way?"

"Superfluous. Wasteful expenditure of words. When you are out, you are out. Sayonara. Aufwiedersehen. Bah-Bye. A warning: anyone trying to illegally escape over the hedge walls will be immediately and forever clipped and eliminated on the spot. On your mark. Get set. Go."

Alice took a deep breath and ran. Animals and birds of every shape and size ran willy-nilly, pushing and shoving like cattle. Alice was caught in the middle. She was moved along with the stampeding crowd. She could barely breathe.

At the first dead end, the sign read All Customer Service Gobbets. The red neon finger flashed as the loud speaker intoned, "This means your job has been outsourced to Bindia." A whole group immediately disappeared, but Alice was safe and she ran on.

The next dead end read Replaced by Consultants, and again the finger flashed and the voice proclaimed, "We no longer have to pay benefits," and another huge group disappeared.

She ran on, in and out of more dead ends and

roadblocks. The finger pointed and the voice intoned, "All Paper Manufacturers exit while we ship your jobs to Chimichangamexicana. Olé!"

At the Past Your Prime and Expiration Date sign, a group of retirees vanished.

One dead end had a special door reading Upper Level Execs Exit Here. This group was escorted out in a very polite, orderly fashion with handshakes and pats on the back while being handed checks of varying amounts in one- to twenty-million-dollar denominations as their exit bonus for early dismissal.

Suddenly, the maze opened onto a grassy path. Alice hiked up her skirt, put boot leather to the grass, and ran. She ran harder than when she had run after the rabbit *into* the paper pit, harder than when she had escaped *from* the paper pit, harder even than when she had run *with* the duchess. Her feet were faster than spinning wheels.

She ducked. She dodged. She puffed. She panted. She ran into animals running every which way and hoped she could stay hidden in the crowd. Suddenly, she spied a small opening in the tall privet hedge. She let a large group of animals run past her. No one was watching. She charged through the small opening, scratching her face and arms and tearing her skirt. She heard the loudspeaker shouting "Halt! The neon sign did not give you the finger. Guards, the Alice human has escaped."

She ran on and on down a barely used path in the grass, looking over her shoulder. She expelled a held breath. So far no one was following her. She halted abruptly in front of a giant fence made of glass that blocked the path. There was no way around it. It seemed to stretch from one horizon to the other. Suddenly, smoke drifted over the face of the glass, covering it completely. It disappeared and then reappeared. This must be the smoke-and-mirror fence she had seen when she overlooked Corporateland grounds. What now?

At one point when the smoke cleared and the glass was again visible, she rapped her knuckles against it. It was solid like the glass blocks used in bathrooms for privacy but was also a mirror that reflected her hair hanging in limp sweaty clumps. No more cute shag. Her skirt and sweater looked like she'd been doing serious hard labor. Her scarf hung in tatters. Her stockings were ruined. Her boots were scratched, scuffed and torn beyond ever being wearable again. Magically, all of her donut-dipping weight had disappeared.

A sign on the other side of the glass read DNE e-Zam e-Car. *Now what does that mean? What's an e-car?* She fanned her palm against the hard surface and then cupped her hands on either side of her face and pressed it against the glass in an attempt to see through. She got very excited. The letters on that same sign reversed themselves. END maZ-e raC-e. End Maze Race! But maybe she was seeing things. She stepped back, and the glass was a mirror again with the backward letters. She pressed her face to the glass and it was a window. Again the sign read End Maze Race. This had to be the way out. *I did make it to the end of the maze*, she thought as excitement bubbled through her.

She looked deeper into the space on the other side of the glass. A lime-green aerodynamically shaped vehicle was parked by the station sign: e-Platform. Would the car take her somewhere? Signs hung all over the platform's overhead struts: You Have a Place on the World Wide Web. Sky's the Limit. All Kinds of Possibilities. Opportunity Knocks. Work for Yourself. All with arrows pointing northeast beyond the platform. Now how to get to the other side? It was so close, but so far. She closed her eyes and laid her dejected head against the glass.

All of her breath let go in one big swoosh. Any advantage she'd gained was lost as she heard the trooping of the guards' boots coming nearer and their

shouts, which became a roar in unison. "Halt! You have exited before your time."

If only, if only she could just walk through this glass. Her mind darted frantically, searching for a solution. Going back was not an option. The guards' roar now sounded like thunder. They were closing in. The fence stretched to the horizon on either side and might take her some place, but tired as she was, she doubted she could outrun them. Going forward seemed impossible. "Psst," the voice from her dream whispered in her ear. "Remember, you just have to believe there is no barrier."

"What do I have to lose?" she said.

The voice in her ear rose from a whisper to a shout. "Your head, if you stay here!"

In that next moment, she closed her eyes and pretended that the glass was soft as gauze. Then, suddenly, the glass began to melt away, and the smoke followed into the opening as if pointing the way. Her fingers and then her whole hand melted into the glass. She gasped. The guards were steps away. She could hear them panting and the rattle of their swords.

She felt one grab hold of one of her boots. She pushed her arm through. The glass felt like warm silvery water. As she tried to push her whole body through, a guard latched onto her other boot. Alice's arms flailed, searching for a handhold, and connected with the signpost that said End Maze Race. She gripped her arms around it to haul the rest of her body through. The guards yanked back. She worked one foot free from her boot and flicked it back. The guard whined, "She gave me a bloody nose." One final heave of her arms and another foot thrust, and she was out of the other boot. She landed in a heap at the base of the signpost. She turned and looked back. The liquid glass was again a solid block. Two guards, each clutching one of her boots, looked back and forth at the boots and at Alice as though they couldn't believe that Alice's feet were not in them.

The duchess shouted, "After her." The guards ran at the glass, expecting to travel through, but instead they smashed stunned bodies against the solid glass. They waved their arms and shouted angrily. The duchess joined them in a red-faced rant, mouthing the words "off with her head," but the sound was muted from Alice's side of the glass.

On impulse, Alice pushed her index finger through. The glass was again liquid. A gardener tried to clip her finger with his hedge clippers. She quickly yanked it back. The guards and gardeners banged their fists and swords and head trimmers against the wall, but it was impenetrable. She could go back and forth. They couldn't. "You can have my corporate head. I don't want it anymore," she mouthed back from her side of the glass.

Taking no chances, she hopped in the lime-green car. The driver was a pretty, dark-haired woman dressed in black pants, a pink flowered blouse, and a melon-colored jacket. In a voice filled with cheerful confidence, she said, "Destination, please."

"Put distance between them and me, just in case they find a way through," Alice urged.

The car zipped along so quickly and traveled so far that the looking glass out the back window of the car was only a small shiny piece that the sun caught in the distance.

"I've been where you've been," the driver said. "Now this is my business," she said, patting the dashboard of the car. Her voice was both cheerful and compassionate. "When you've had time to rest and think about where you are going next, you might want to consider this." She reached across the seat and handed Alice a business card. It read, **"**Work from Home on the Internet. Be Your Own Boss. Call me."

"You seem human and you sound human, but I'm exhausted. I can't even think about someone else telling me where to go," Alice said. The card fluttered to the floor. She curled up on the back seat and fell sound asleep. The driver looked back and smiled a knowing smile. She reached over the seat and tucked another business card securely between Alice's hands, which were palmed together under her head.

Alice had no idea how long she had been sleeping, but when she woke up and stretched, instead of the leather backseat of the car, she felt the smooth damask of her very own couch in her own home in front of her fireplace. She blinked her eyes, expecting it to disappear. It *was* her home, yet it looked different. She couldn't put a finger on it. She was in the same place, but wasn't. She wiggled her bare toes. No high-heeled boots. She was never wearing high heels again. She smoothed her skirt and sweater, which were clean, but the skirt had a slight rip at the waistline. She excitedly fingered her waist; she was slimmer and trimmer than before!

She rubbed her eyes. She gazed above the fireplace and blinked rapidly. The mirror hung over the fireplace just like before, but it looked strangely like the looking glass she'd just traveled through.

It must have all been a very bad dream. She stood up, and a business card fluttered to the floor. She plucked a privet hedge twig from inside her sweater sleeve.

She squinted and thought she saw the duchess and the guards shaking their fists at her in the mirror, but it was like a picture of a distant landscape. She squinted again, and their figures became teeny tiny miniatures like toys. She blinked and they were gone.

The Beginning ... but that's another story!

Acknowledgements

A special heartfelt thank-you to Shirley Britton for creative consultation and for an enduring friendship. What we do best: fine dining over wine and wisdom while playing with the creative building blocks of life.

To Doris Miller for her delightful illustrations that added just the right touch.

I'm grateful to practically every company for whom I have worked, not only for the source material but for the salary that paid the mortgage and kept shoes on my feet. Some of the best managers I've had have been women and some have been men. The same could be said of the worst.

The Editoral Staff at iUniverse gave me a whole education on how to be a better writer. The finished product would not be the same without them.

Kathi Wittcamper with iUniverse was helpful, positive, and supportive while clearly explaining services.

Early on Suzanne Paulson shared her experiences. The "Butter Both Sides of Your Bread Consultants" reference was derived from a letter left behind at a table where Karen Nowosell was waitressing. Ironically, it pertained to the CEO of the company where I was working at the time.

To Jan Weren for being a computer angel.

Also to Sue Bachman, creative photographer, and another computer angel.

To the STARS—for creative comaraderie, support and just plain fun! Fred Bachman, Janet Beatty, Dorothy Jackson, Beth Keithly, Sandi McCash, Cindy Murphy, Phyllis Rodenhouse, Susan Ryan, and the "executive committee"—Barbara Woods and Pat Zapal!

Other thanks go to Chris Cook, Paul Davids, Lise Marinelli, Bonnie Norris, Whitney Scott, and Robert Hendricks.

On a personal note, thanks to the "Breakfast Club" for welcoming me so warmly when I moved to South Haven: Jake and Bea Hudson, Shelly and Bernadine Gould, Peter Hawkins, Elaine Troehler, Elle Troehler, Mike and Peggy Gould, Lindsey and Larry Gould, and assorted friends and relatives who drop by for Sunday breakfast.

Artist's Bio

Illustrator, Doris Miller, is a graduate of Western Michigan University and a retired art administrator from the Kalamazoo, Michigan, public schools.

Awards she has received: The Community Medal of Arts, Michigan Art Educator of the Year, Kalamazoo Public Schools Adminstrator of the Year, Excellence in Teaching Award, and Western Michigan University 100 Outstanding Art Alumni.

At the West Michigan Cancer Center, she coordinates an art therapy program and art exhibitions, and has illustrated a cookbook for cancer patients. She exhibits and sells her painting in South Haven and Kalamazoo, Michigan.